FAVOURITE SONG

COMPILATION OF SHORT SCREENPLAYS AWARDED AT INTERNATIONAL FILM FESTIVALS

BY

KATARZYNA ADAMUS

161 DAYS 2020

161 Days

Fulfil your dreams

161 Days

Fulfil your dreams

ISBN 9781912831340

CONTENTS

Dear Reader,

I decided to publish my short screenplays encouraged by numerous questions, where is possible to read my works. So here they are!

These short scripts won multiple awards at the international film festivals.

I was born in Poland and English is my second language, so there are tiny mistakes sometimes in the projects.

If you are interested to produce one of these scripts, please contact me. You can find me on IMDb.

<u>EXHIBITION</u>

Written by

Katarzyna Adamus
(K.E.Adamus)

DRAFT
2

FADE IN

INT. DAY. ART GALLERY "MERMAID"

Elegantly but extravagantly dressed Maria looks at one of
the paintings and sipping free wine. The gallery owner
approaches her.

                    THE GALLERY OWNER

          A beautiful painting, isn't it?

                    MARIA

          I'm just watching, sorry!

Maria puts down a glass of wine and runs away.

                    THE GALLERY OWNER

          See you again on the next exhibition!

INT. EVENING. MARIA AND HENRY'S HOUSE.

Maria is coming into her house. She takes off her purple
coat in the hallway. Henry's voice can be heard.

                    HENRY

          Where have you been?

                    MARIA
          I went for a walk.

Maria enters the room where Henry, middle aged man with
beard grown, sits on the couch, with a glass of whiskey in
his hand, watching the western.

                    HENRY
          Have you captured anything
          interesting? You and those photos!

                    MARIA
          I think the owner of the art gallery
          thought I wanted to buy something. I
          didn't have time to take any
          pictures.

                    HENRY
          So we're going to the galleries
          again! You and art, ha-ha-ha. You and
          buying art! Yes! That's even better!

Loud knocking to the doors.

                    HENRY (cont'd)
          If someone asks, I'm not at home!

Maria opens the door. A chunky man is standing outside.

                    THE BAILIFF
          Can I speak to Mr Henry?

                    MARIA
          He is not at home.

                    THE BAILIFF
          It's even better. That also concerns
          you.

He hands her an envelope and leaves. Maria comes back, with
the envelope in her hand. She sits down on the kitchen
floor, takes out the official letter from the envelope and
starts reading it.

We can hear Henry's voice.

                    HENRY
          Who was it?

Maria does not answer. Henry enters the kitchen.

                    MARIA
          Why did you pledge the house? Where
          did you get that loan from? For what?

                    HENRY
          My house, my loan, my business!

Henry leaves the kitchen. You can hear the door slamming.

INT. DAY. ART SHOP

Maria is looking at sets of brushes and oil paints.

                    SHOP ASSISTANT
          Can I help you?

                    MARIA
          I have forgotten what it takes to
          paint a picture!

                    SHOP ASSISTANT
          I'd be happy to help. For starters a
          small canvas size might be good.

                    MARIA
          It is a gift for the artist and it
          must be a big format, because the
          name is big!

The salesman reaches for a large canvas, burying in brushes
and paints, choosing the right materials.

                    SHOP ASSISTANT
          Well, then you will need this... And
          this... What's the artist's name? If
          I may know?

                    MARIA
          Churchill... Henry Churchill...

The salesman looks confused.

                    SHOP ASSISTANT
          Yes, it rings the bell!

                    MARIA
          No doubts!

The salesman quickly packs things. Maria starts to dig
nervously in her wallet.

                    SHOP ASSISTANT
          It will be 100 pounds altogether.

                    MARIA
          How much?

                    SHOP ASSISTANT
          Yes, you are lucky, we have a
          Valentines' sale at the moment!

Maria's taking some change out of her wallet. Finally, she
takes out her credit card and nervously pays for shopping.

INT. DAY. MARIA AND HENRY'S HOUSE.

Maria enters the room where Henry smokes a cigarette while
watching the western. We can hear "Harmonica man" from the
movie "Once upon a time in wild west".

                    HENRY
          Do you hear this? Listen to this!
          This is called music!

Maria hands him a package from the artists' shop.

                    MARIA
          Now listen to me! If there's no
          picture by tomorrow, there won't be
          me either!

Henry turns to the cat, which is warming up by the radiator.

                    HENRY
          Cat! The missus got nervous!

Maria breathes heavily out of her anger and runs out of the
room. Henry is curious to unpack the package. When he sees
objects to paint, his face changes. He grabs the remote and
switches the channel to pop music.

INT. MORNING. MARIA AND HENRY'S HOUSE.

Maria is calling the bank where Henry took a loan.

                    MARIA
          Is there really nothing you can do?

                    CLERK
          If Mr. Henry had come in a few months
          ago... Now, unfortunately, it's too
          late.

Henry runs into the kitchen, wearing the same clothes as
yesterday, stained with oil paints.

Maria is disconnecting the phone call.

                    HENRY
          Come with me, check it out! You
          always doubted in me!

                    MARIA
          Me?

                              HENRY
                   Yes, it's you who I'm talking to.
                   Come with me!

He runs out of the kitchen and goes to the TV room. There's
a portrait of a beautiful young woman, set up on the easel.
Maria looks in silence for a while. She starts screaming.

                              MARIA
                   Who is it? Is that the slut you took
                   the loan for? Because it wasn't for
                   me!

Henry starts silently packing his things. He makes a phone
call in the kitchen. Maria is still looking at the picture.

Henry enters the TV room.

                              HENRY
                   I'm going to the countryside. We're
                   gonna take a break. You became too
                   nervous recently!

                              MARIA
                   How arty it is! To make a mess and
                   disappear!

                              HENRY
                   You was always jealous about my
                   talent. Always!

He leaves the house. Maria sees through the window a woman,
resembling the one from the portrait, approaching in the
car. Henry gets in to the car.

INT. DAY. "THE BEST ART" ART GALLERY.

Maria is showing to the manger of the gallery the picture
painted by Henry.

                              GALLERY MANAGER
                   Cool, nice. How many of them do you
                   have?

                              MARIA
                   What do you mean by "how many"?

                              GALLERY MANAGER
                   If you don't have a large collection,
                   we won't talk... You see how much
                   space you have here?
                              (MORE)

                    GALLERY MANAGER (cont'd)
          One painting doesn't satisfy me. Not
          at all, even though it's a good one.

INT. EVENING. MARIA AND HENRY'S HOUSE.

Maria sits on the couch with her legs curled up and drinks
wine. She's watching the movie "The Forger". You can see the
scene when the film's protagonist starts to paint his copy
and creates it. Maria starts crying. She puts the glass down
and takes out the bailiff letter, reading it again. She
stops crying. She reaches for the glass and drinks the rest
of the wine in one go.

INT. MORNING. MARIA AND HENRY'S HOUSE.

You can see a disturbed cat rubbing against Maria's hand,
hanging from the couch, next to the empty bottle of wine and
a big red stain on the floor. After a while the hand moves.
Maria gets up, you can see that she has a powerful hangover.
She speaks to the cat.

                    MARIA
          Don't worry, the missus will figure
          out something. This is our house too,
          mine and yours.

INT. DAY. MARIA AND HENRY'S HOUSE.

Maria sets up the easel and starts painting. Unfortunately,
it doesn't seem to work for her. She looks at her work ,
turning head into different angles, with big dislike seen on
her face. Discouraged, she cleans her hands of paint and
reaches for the phone. She calls her daughter and speaks to
her.

                    MARIA
          I forgot how to paint. The years of
          no training are doing their job.

                    MARIA'S DAUGHTER
          And it's probably my fault, because
          when I was born, you stopped to
          paint. You're still with that fraud
          man?

                    MARIA
          He left...

                    MARIA'S DAUGHTER
          That's good news! You will be better
          on your own. I've seen your work
          once. Those oil paintings weren't
          good...

Maria interrupts.

                         MARIA
          Thank you for the encouragement. I
          have to draw nineteen paintings in a
          week and sell or they'll take our
          house! I need money for first
          installment!

                    MARIA'S DAUGHTER
          You know that oil painting was never
          your strength, but...

We can see that Maria face lighten up with optimism.

INT. DAY. MARIA AND HENRY'S HOUSE.

Maria and her daughter are looking through Maria's drawings,
painted with specialist markers.

                    MARIA'S DAUGHTER
          I'll take a few photo shots of each
          drawing, you can sell prints on the
          Internet.

                         MARIA
          Will someone buy it?

                    MARIA'S DAUGHTER
          We'll see. You may become famous
          after you die. You know what it's
          like in the art world.

Maria sighs and watches her daughter photographing pictures.

INT. DAY. "THE BEST ART" ART GALLERY.

The gallery manager reviews Maria's drawings, shaking his
head.

                    GALLERY MANAGER
          You can't sell it here. Maybe on the
          Internet, but I doubt it either.
          Nice, but unsaleable... I'm sorry.

The gallery manager gives back to Maria a portfolio filled
with drawings.

INT. DAY. ART GALLERY "MERMAID"

The owner is silently reviewing Maria's work.

                    THE GALLERY OWNER
          It's gonna be hard to sell. It's your
          job, right? I always knew you were
          some kind of talented artist. It's
          just a little unusual kind of art...

Maria reaches for the portfolio, held by the gallery owner.

                    MARIA
          I understand.

The gallery owner does not want to give back portfolio. She
starts reviewing it again.

                    THE GALLERY OWNER
          You know what? I have a gap - just
          one week. I wanted to do a photo
          exhibition of a young artist, but
          he's still delaying, not answering my
          calls. He probably hasn't taken the
          pictures yet. The artist, you know...
          Well, I'm on it! One week.

                    MARIA
          Thank you very much. You don't even
          know how much I'm thankful!

INT. EVENING. MARIA AND HENRY'S HOUSE.

Maria is on the phone with her daughter.

                    MARIA
          Yeah, they're picking up the works
          tomorrow... All framed and ready! You
          don't even know...

You can hear the door slamming. Maria stops the
conversation. You can hear the steps in the hallway and the
kitchen. After a while, Henry appears in the room, holding
some pictures of Maria, framed and behind glass.

                    HENRY
          Do you really think you'll ever
          become a painter? Don't you see it's
          shit? Be reasonable!

                    MARIA
          Artists don't have to be reasonable!

                    HENRY
          After all, it's shit.

Henry throws pictures at the coffee table. The glass breaks,
crippling the pictures. Maria throws a cup of coffee at
Henry. He bounces the mug that lands on the pictures,
flooding them with coffee.

                    HENRY (cont'd)
          Pathology! But what could I expect
          from someone with only a secondary
          education. Will you throw a knife at
          me too?

                    MARIA
          You'll see!

Maria runs to the kitchen and grabs the big chopper. Henry
runs away from the house. You can hear the sound of him
running down the stairs, the sound of the fall, the curse.
Maria puts the chopper away and looks out through the window
at Henry, getting into the same car as previously. Maria
sits down at the floor and starts crying.

INT. EVENING. HOUSE OF MARIA'S DAUGHTER

Maria's daughter is looking at her mother, who is sitting on
the floor, with the face hidden behind the palms.

                    MARIA'S DAUGHTER
          What's all the fuss about? Was it
          supposed to be a photo exhibition? It
          will be!

                    MARIA
          And you, Brutus, against me? You too?

                    MARIA'S DAUGHTER
          I took pictures of your work, don't
          you remember? The prints came in
          today, and they're even bigger than
          originals. All you have to do is to
          buy set of bigger frames!

                         MARIA
          I don't have the money anymore!

                    MARIA'S DAUGHTER
          Don't worry, we'll figure something
          out!

INT. EVENING. ART GALLERY "MERMAID"

Maria stands in front of a photograph of one of her
pictures, framed in a handmade frame. A handsome man
approaches her.

                     HANDSOME MAN
          Just watching? They always give good
          wine at the openings here.

                         MARIA

          Not anymore!

We see a surprised look on the man's face. He leaves her
disgusted. The owner of the gallery approaches Maria.

                    THE GALLERY OWNER
          I knew there was something about you.
          A buyer is interested in your work.
          Come with me, let me introduce you...

FADE OUT

EYE FOR EYE

Written by

<u>K. E. Adamus</u>
(Katarzyna Adamus)

Draft
2

INT. HOUSE OF ERIK. KITCHEN. DAY

Erik, a man in his 60s, is kneading the dough with his hands. The dough sticks to all his fingers.

                    ERIK
          Oh, for fuck sake!

His phone starts to ring. Erik hesitates, looking at his palms with all the dough on it. Then he answer the phone, messing it all with the cake.

                    ERIK (cont'd)
          What? I hope it is worth it!

                    MAGGIE
          Did you sign the papers?

                    ERIK
          The whole world is on fire, and you
          think about us? How is it possible?

                    MAGGIE
          You, and your sarcasm. Margaret told
          me, that you bought an axe. I can
          guess what will be next!

                    ERIK
          Yes? Tell me...

                    MAGGIE
          You will be in your own world for
          next few months! Sign the papers! We
          are over!

                    ERIK
          I'm trying to do some bread here. It
          is not the best time.

                    MAGGIE
          You work from home again?

                    ERIK
          It is not home anymore, without
          you...

We can hear sound of hanging out. Erik is looking at the phone, then he puts it aside and start to knead the dough with fury. He gradually calms down.

INT. ERIK'S HOUSE. KITCHEN. DAY.

Erik is looking through the glass of the oven at the baking bread.

                         ERIK
          Come on, you lucky bastard! Grow!

Erik takes the phone and start to ring someone. Nobody answers. He chooses the next number. Again, nobody answers.

                         ERIK (cont'd)
          Corona holidays! Fucking people!

Suddenly the phone rings. Erik is looking at the name of calling person. He is going to put the phone aside, then he changes his mind and answers.

                         ERIK (cont'd)
          You have balls, I have to admit this,
          you have balls.

                         PETER
          I will pop up with the papers to
          sign. You probably lost last them.
          Like the previous ones.

                         ERIK
          You can get lost! With all viruses in
          the world!

                         PETER
          Let's face it, she has chosen me!

                         ERIK
          Fuck off! Come here and you will see
          my real face, my real myself! You
          will leave in the ambulance!

                         PETER
          Ha, ha! You are always strong in your
          mouth. See you soon.

Erik puts the phone aside and starts to watch the bread.

                         ERIK
          Fucking asshole! You fucking asshole!

Suddenly we can hear single beep from fire alarm in the lounge. Erik freeze. After few seconds the beep repeats.

Erik opens the oven, but there is no smoke. He opens the window.

INT. ERIK'S HOUSE. LOUNGE. DAY. FEW MINUTES LATER.

Erik is on the phone. During chat we can hear single beeps from the fire alarm.

                    TOM
          Dad, sign these papers. I am fed up
          with all of this. Monica cought the
          virus.

                    ERIK
          Who's Monica?

                    TOM
          Just sign the papers. Mum is planning
          section you.

                    ERIK
          Ha, ha! I am the shrink! I can
          section her!

                    TOM
          We both know she has all the grounds
          for it. You behaviour was...

                    ERIK
          Yes?

                    TOM
          Just sign the papers. I am worried
          about you! I heard you bought an axe.

                    ERIK
          The world is not stable. There might
          be electricity gaps. I like to drink
          my coffee in the morning.

                    TOM
          So why the axe? I don't follow you.

                    ERIK
          I have survival camping thing, to
          make a fire. The axe? I will get rid
          of this fucking tree, which council
          forbade to cut.

                    TOM
          Trees are important to ecosystem!

                    ERIK
          I have no light in my fucking study
          room! I need vitamin D!

                         TOM
          Dad, they will lock you finally!

After a moment of silence.

                         TOM (cont'd)
          Dad, what is this sound?

                         ERIK
          What sound?

                         TOM
          The beeping sound.

                         ERIK
          It is just my private bomb. Listen, I
          am baking first bread in my life,
          would you like to...

                         TOM
          Oh my God! Oh my God!

We can hear sound of ended connection. Erik starts to surf
in the Internet.

INT. ERIK'S HOUSE. LOUNGE. DAY. FEW MINUTES LATER.

Erik is standing on the chair under the beeping fire alarm.

Erik start to talk aloud.

                         ERIK
          Reset. Fucking reset. There is no
          fucking reset button here!

He switches the "check" button and presses it for few
seconds. We can hear loud sound of fire alarm. Erik releases
the button. After few seconds the alarm stops to ring, then
we can hear again the single beeps in regular intervals.

We can hear knocking to the door.

INT./EXT. AT THE DOOR OF ERIK'S HOUSE. DAY.

Erik opens the door. There is a policeman outside.

                         THE POLICEMAN
          What's this noise?

                    ERIK
          What noise? The neighbours, they are
          liars! I am the most quiet person on
          this street!

                    THE POLICEMAN
          The noise...

                    ERIK
          How much noise you can do, while
          reading and writing?

                    THE POLICEMAN
          Someone just reported you have a bomb
          here.

Erik starts to laugh.

                    ERIK
          God bless you! You came alone to the
          suspect with the bomb!

                    THE POLICEMAN
          What is this noise?

                    ERIK
          It is just a dying fire alarm. The
          battery to be correct.

                    THE POLICEMAN
          Get rid of it. It is disturbing. You
          have to think about your community.

                    ERIK
          My community? My community bought
          everything from the shop! There are
          empty shelves! How I will get
          replacement battery? Who will fix it?
          All people are sitting at homes,
          scared to death!

                    THE POLICEMAN
          I understand your concern. Just
          please get rid of the noise.

                    ERIK
          My bread!

He leaves the policeman and runs to the kitchen.

INT. ERIK'S HOUSE. KITCHEN. DAY.

Erik opens the oven and gets out a brown loaf of fresh bread.

                    ERIK
          Just in the last moment!

We can hear voice of the policeman.

                    THE POLICEMAN
          Can I come in?

                    ERIK
          Yeah, I will share some bread.

INT. ERIK'S HOUSE. LOUNGE. DAY. FEW MINUTES LATER.

Erik and the policeman are sitting on the sofa and eating the bread. It looks like they were sitting and chatting for a while.

                    THE POLICEMAN
          I would sign the papers. She's the
          bitch.

                    ERIK
          I won't! Never! She is my wife!

                    THE POLICEMAN
          I have to go. Get rid of this noise.
          Otherwise we will get lots of calls
          from neighborhood. We do not need it
          at the moment. We have more serious
          crimes.

                    ERIK
          Thank you, officer. I will do.

INT. ERIK'S HOUSE. LOUNGE. DAY. FEW MINUTES LATER.

Erik is standing on the chair. He makes a cross sign in the air and crashes the alarm appliance with the axe. The electricity goes through the axe and gives him small electric shock. The part of alarm appliance flies towards the doors, just to hit in the eye Peter, who just entered without knocking.

Erik is falling on the floor. The falling axe cuts his toe.

Peter is slowly sitting on the floor, keeping the rest of his eye. We can hear the sound of approaching car and voice of The policeman.

                    THE POLICEMAN
          I forgot my cap!

INT. HOSPITAL. EVENING. A&E SECTION.

Peter and Erik are laying on the beds, situated next to each other. Between them there is Maggie, sitting in silence on the stool. The policeman is taking their statements.

                    THE POLICEMAN
          OK, guys. That's all for now. It has
          been not pleasant accident. I hope
          someone will help you soon.

                    PETER
          It's been three hours! And we are
          still waiting! My fucking eye! Oh my
          God!

                    ERIK
          You should knock on the doors! Times
          when you could just pop up are over.

                    PETER
          You are lucky, you fucking prick! You
          would die there on the floor!

                    ERIK
          Than you would not need the papers.
          She would be yours. Fuck it! I will
          sign them now. Thanks that you freed
          me from this ... accompany!

                    MAGGIE
          Now? Now you are paralyzed! how are
          you going to sign? How are you going
          to pay the mortgage?

                    THE POLICEMAN
          I told you something before...

                    ERIK
          Yeah, I remember. Now I see, you was
          right.

                    PETER
          Maggie, will you still love me
          without an eye? I will get a sick
          benefits, we will be OK.

Erik starts to laugh.

                    ERIK
          You can still work with one eye, you
          lazy cunt. If I was able, I would
          treat you properly with this axe!

                    THE POLICEMAN
          Stay calm, gentlemen.

                    MAGGIE
               (to the policeman)
          What? You just heard what he said!

                    THE POLICEMAN
          You have rights to sue him later. It
          is up to you. He clearly can not do
          anything, so his threatening is just
          talking.

The nurse approaches. She speaks to Maggie.

                    THE NURSE
          You need to leave. Only the relatives
          can stay now in this section.

                    ERIK
          She's my wife.

                    PETER
          Fuck you!

                    THE NURSE
          I have in my papers that Mrs Maggie
          Gregorson is with Mr Peter Schmidt.
          Is that correct?

                    ERIK
          Yeah, but she still is my wife.

Maggie takes out from her handbag papers, stained with
blood.

                    MAGGIE
          Just sign it!

Peter takes his left hand and gets a ball point and papers.

He signs the papers with his initials.

                    ERIK
          Happy?

Peter is looking at them with his one eye. The second eye is
behind the dressing.

                    PETER
          I do not want her anymore.

                    ERIK
          Me either!

Peter starts to laugh.

                    PETER
          We would be even if it was on
          purpose, but you lost your eye due to
          the accident.

                    ERIK
          It's not lost yet!

                    PETER
          It is!

                    MAGGIE
          Nurse! Do something about it!

                    THE NURSE
          Madam, you need to leave according to
          latest policy...

                    MAGGIE
          I would like to speak to your
          manager!

                    THE POLICEMAN
          I will show you the way...

                    MAGGIE
          How can you know it?

                    THE POLICEMAN
          ...to the nearest exit. I have good
          orientation skills. Let's go.

The Policeman and Maggie leave the ward. The Nurse starts
filling the reports.

                    ERIK
You was never a good friend. Good
friends do not steal wives.

                    PETER
It does not count, she is a witch! I
did not know, that you were paying
her mortgage...

                    ERIK
Car as well.

                    PETER
I don't feel comfortable with this
knowledge. She can go to hell. Are we
even?

                    ERIK
If you have problem, you can use my
expertise. I'm well experienced in
treating all kind of drama.

                    PETER
Do you also treat your patients with
the axe?

                    ERIK
No, they passed this knowledge on me.

                    PETER
How much do you charge?

                    ERIK
Too much for you.

                    PETER
I guess it will never be same again.

                    ERIK
No man, it won't. It won't.

Fade out.

                    THE END

Favourite song

Written by

Katarzyna Adamus

2

Fade in

EXT. THE BEACH. EARLY EVENING.

Two obese, middle aged women, ANNA and KATE, and one obese
man, VLAD, in similar age, are sitting on the beach. They
are drinking whiskey, shouting and singing. Anna takes out
the phone and puts on the music.

                         VLAD
              Next song is mine!

                         ANNA
              What do you mean? You have your own
              phone!

                         VLAD
              My battery is flat!

                         KATE
              Shhh! Be quiet!

                         ANNA
              What do you mean? Be quiet! Oh
              please!

                         KATE
              We shouldn't be here.

                         ANNA
              So what?

                         KATE
              The police is patrolling the area!

                         ANNA
              So what?

                         KATE
              I'm broke and I don't have money for
              penalty tickets!

                         VLAD
              It's not working like this. Not here.
              Not in the UK. Firstly, they are
              giving you a warning...

                         KATE
              I had a warning two days ago.

All of them start to laugh.

                    VLAD
          I can't laugh anymore! My belly!

                    ANNA
          It's bigger than week ago.

                    VLAD
          Look at yours!

                    KATE
          Mine is same!

                    ANNA
          It's because you are lazy! You need
          sport!

                    KATE
          I'm not lazy! I'm depressed!

                    VLAD
          If police will come, we are telling
          them, that we took you for a walk,
          because you have a depression!

                    KATE
          Deal!

They stop conversation.

                    KATE (cont'd)
          Listen to the waves sound!

                    ANNA
          And you wanted to sit at house, like
          in the grave. We all might be dead
          tomorrow! Use your life!

                    KATE
          I have lot's of remote work.

                    ANNA
          Fuck it!

                    VLAD
          Fuck it!

                    KATE
          Cheers!

They start to drink again.

                    VLAD
          Anna, I want my favourite song!

                    ANNA
          What is your favourite song?

                    VLAD
          I forgot the title and the band name.
          Give me your phone, I will google
          some words...

                    ANNA
          Maybe later. Let's go to the harbour!

They are getting up and walking inside the harbour.

EXT. HARBOUR. LATE EVENING

There is no water in the harbour because of the low tide.
The ground is muddy and slippery. During they walk they fall
down often, laughing. They take some pictures of the boats,
laying on the ground, and of themselves.

                    VLAD
          Anna, I want my favourite song!

                    ANNA
          No!

                    KATE
          You need to bribe her!

                    VLAD
          Anna, I will buy you pizza.

                    ANNA
          No!

                    KATE
          Vlad, she likes abandoned places!

Anna starts to laugh.

                    ANNA
          Kate, you are a bitch!

                    VLAD
          Anna, I know some place. You will
          literally shit yourself there.

                    ANNA
          Where is it?

                    VLAD
          Firstly, my song!

                    ANNA
You don't even know what is it!

                    VLAD
Just give me your phone for few
minutes.

                    ANNA
Firstly tell me about this place!

                    VLAD
We can go there now! I have a car!

                    KATE
We can't go like this! We are all
drunk!

                    ANNA
So what? I am working in the
hospital. I can die now anytime.

                    KATE
We did not eat anything. On empty
stomach all of this alcohol will go
straight to the head and we will
crash.

                    VLAD
I can order a pizza. I have discount!
Kate, do you have phone?

                    KATE
10 percent of battery.

                    VLAD
It should be enough.

Vlad takes the phone from Kate and starts to call.

                    VLAD (cont'd)
Hi, can speak to the manager? Hi
Darren! Can I order two vegetarian
pizzas? I am with two girls! One is a
nurse, she has Covid-19 and is on
quarantine, but we are in the
harbour. Second one just escaped from
some mental asylum. Yes! With a
discount. Do you still have details
of my card? Great! Is it done? Now
listen, one more pizza pepperoni.
Darren? Darren? Fucking battery!

                    KATE
Will he come?

                    VLAD
He has to, I already paid!

EXT. HARBOUR. LATE EVENING

Anna, Kate and Vlad are sitting on the bench facing the
harbour. They are all covered in the mud from the harbour.

                    KATE
We should not sit here. It is three
of us. Noone will believe we are
family. We look similar with all this
mud coverage, but still...

                    VLAD
You will get another warning!

                    KATE
I prefer to keep this opportunity for
tomorrow. I have a date.

                    ANNA
With whom?

                    KATE
You don't know him.

                    VLAD
OK, you two exchange some gossips and
I am going to the toilet.

Vlad goes away, into nearby bushes. Suddenly a pizza car
appears. Anna starts to wave at them. The car stops, and
PIZZA DRIVER gets out of the car.

                    ANNA
I'm the nurse, Vlad told you about.
He will be right back. Just went to
the loo.

                    PIZZA DRIVER
You are on quarantine?

                    ANNA
No, not now. I am working again since
a week.

Pizza driver takes out the food from his bag. We see two big boxes and one very small. Pizza driver leaves it at the nearby bench.

>   PIZZA DRIVER
>   Enjoy your meal!

Pizza driver drives away. Vlad is coming back and spotting small pizza.

>   VLAD
>   I will kill him! Is it a joke? Anna,
>   give me your phone!

Anna hands in her phone to Vlad.

>   ANNA
>   No music!

Vlad starts to call.

>   VLAD
>   Hi, I would like to speak to the
>   manager. What do you mean he is gone?

Vlad gives back phone to Anna.

>   VLAD (cont'd)
>   He said he got covid - 19 from you
>   and went home for quarantine. Look at
>   this, is this my pepperoni?

He opens the tiny box. His pepperoni pizza is very small.

>   VLAD (cont'd)
>   I will kill him.

>   ANNA
>   Relax. We have two big pizzas.

Vlad takes on of the boxes. Pizza falls out of it and ends up on the ground. Out of nowhere seagulls appear and start to eat the pizza.

>   VLAD
>   Great! I lost appetite!

>   ANNA
>   Eat! You promised we are going to
>   this abandoned place! What is it
>   exactly?

They swap bench, leaving noisy seagulls behind, and share
pizza.

                    VLAD
        It is amazing. I was walking this
        place. There were birds singing, cars
        passing by. And suddenly, with one
        step ahead, it all stopped, It was
        silence like in the outer space. Like
        in the vacuum. Nothing. Not a single
        sound!

                    ANNA
        You joking?

                    VLAD
        No way! It is a real story!

                    KATE
        I am going in the car's boot!

                    VLAD
        You are talking like this, and later
        are surprised, that people are
        avoiding you!

                    KATE
        I prefer to avoid the police. They
        are stopping cars. A couple looks OK,
        but not all of us three. I will hide
        in the car boot. I used to lay there
        few times, as a teenager, when there
        was too many passengers...

                    VLAD
        You, and your stories.

                    ANNA
        It makes sense. Let's go.

EXT. MOTORWAY. NIGHT.

Vlad is driving careless. Sitting next to him Anna is silent
and serious. She looks scared. We can hear shouting from the
boot.

                    KATE
        Stop the car! I do not want another
        car accident! Few times in life is
        enough.

                          VLAD
              We will be fine.

Suddenly a police car appears behind them. It slows down and
then with the signals and lights on force them to stop. Vlad
stops the car. Kate pops out from the boot, looking very
angry. Two policemen run out of the car.

                          MALE POLICEMEN
              Freeze!

Kate stops, confused and raises her hands up. Male
policeman, approaches the car. FEMALE POLICEMAN approaches
Kate.

                          FEMALE POLICEMAN
              You are OK?

                          KATE
              I'm depressed!

                          FEMALE POLICEMAN
              Will be right back!

She approaches the car to back up the Male Policeman

                          MALE POLICEMAN
              Show me your hands! Slowly! Get out
              of the car. Slowly! 01427, we need
              back up!

Policemen get out Anna and Vlad and handcuff them. Kate runs
out into the forest.

                          MALE POLICEMAN (cont'd)
              What the...

                          VLAD
              She was depressed and wanted to go
              for a walk. So we decided to go this
              abandoned place... Where there is
              silence...

                          MALE POLICEMAN
              I will read you your rights!

INT. ANNA'S FLAT. DAY.

Kate and Anna are sitting next to each other and drinking
whiskey.

                    ANNA
          Unbelievable! He had no symptoms! If
          not the police, and a routine check
          up, he would be dead.

                    KATE
          Sooner or later we all will be dead.

                    ANNA
          It is not funny. He is in critical
          state. I saw him yesterday. He is in
          the next ward!

                    KATE
          How is he?

Anna starts to cry.

                    ANNA
          He is on life support machine. He was
          begging me to take him out.

                    KATE
          What did a doctor say?

                    ANNA
          They are going to leave him to die.

                    KATE
          Nonsense!

                    ANNA
          They can't rescue him!

                    KATE
          But we can!

INT. HOSPITAL. DAY.

Anna visits Vlad. Vlad takes out the respirator mask for a
while.

                    VLAD
          I will be fine, just give it to this
          man next to me. He has three kids.

DOCTOR and NURSE approach.

                    DOCTOR
          So we are taking it out!

                         ANNA
          You can't! He is a human being, for
          fuck sake!

                         NURSE
          You know the procedures.

Doctor and nurse takes out the respirator and leave.

                         VLAD
          Assholes!

Anna takes out from the bag male clothes.

                         ANNA
          Dress up! We are going to the beach!

With help of Anna Vlad puts on the clothes. He sits on the
wheelchair. Anna secretly takes him outside, passing the
hospital corridors.

EXT. OUTSIDE OF THE HOSPITAL. DAY.

Kate is waiting on the parking in the car.

                         VLAD
          This time Anna will be in the boot.
          The place is 2 miles away.

                         ANNA
          What place?

                         VLAD
          The place we were going to. I want to
          go there.

Anna gets into the boot. Kate as a driver and Anna as a
passenger drive away.

Vlad is giving directions.

                         VLAD (cont'd)
          Do you see this small bridge? By the
          bridge turn left.

EXT. DEEP FOREST. DAY.

Anna, Kate and Vlad are sitting in the spot, which Vlad was
talking about. There is a complete silence.

                                                KATE
                          Favourite song...

                                                ANNA
                          What favourite song? What do you hear
                          this time?

Vlad starts to laugh, with a horrible cough spasms.

                                                KATE
                          His favourite song.

                                                VLAD
                          Yes, my song!

                                                ANNA
                          What is it? What's the title?

Vlad starts to laugh.

                                          ANNA (cont'd)
                          What's so funny?

                                                VLAD
                          Do you remember this fucking
                          pepperoni pizza?

Vlad starts to laugh and cough. Suddenly the cough stops.
Vlad dies.

Anna and Kate start to cry. The "silence" is still there.

                                                KATE
                          It's his turn to be in the boot, but
                          how we will explain this, when police
                          will stop us?

                                                ANNA
                          Fuck off! He's dead now. And we will
                          never get to know, what was his
                          favourite song!

Fade out

<u>Foursomes</u>

Written by

Katarzyna Adamus

INT. KATIA'S ROOM. DAY.

Katia, Anna and Maggie are sitting on the floor. They are
painting their nails and chatting. They are in their
thirties.

                    ANNA
          How is your dating going on?

                    KATIA
          What dating? I should become a nun
          probably. Thinking of all gossips
          they got more sex each week than me
          for the whole year...

Katia's phone starts to ring.

                    MAGGIE
          Who is it? Answer!

Katia hesitates, then she answers the phone.

                    BEN
          Hi! Can we meet today? I'm in the
          town, free tonight.

                    KATIA
          I can't meet today. I have two
          guests.

                    BEN
          Listen, take your guests and come to
          meet me!

                    KATIA
          No problem, let's meet next to the
          harbour.

                    MAGGIE
          Who was it?

                    KATIA
          Let's get ready! We are going for a
          foursome date. He did not believe I
          have guests, so let him suffer.

EXT. THE STREET NEXT TO HARBOUR. DAY.

Ben is sitting in his car, when Katia with her friends
approaches. Ben looks at them and do not want to get out of
the car. Katia knocks to his window screen.

                         KATIA
               Let's go party!

Ben lowers the window screen.

                         BEN
               I did not sign for this...

                         ANNA
               Let's go party!

Maggie opens the back door of the car. She gets in. After
her Anna. Katia takes her place next to Ben.

INT. PUB. EVENING.

Katia, Ben, Maggie and Anna are playing billards. Girls
order drinks. Ben is paying.

                         BEN
               I will just go to repark the car.

He goes away. Phone of Katia starts to ring. It's Ben.

                         BEN (cont'd)
               Listen, I had some emergency I will
               call you next week.

                         ANNA
               Looks like we scared your boyfriend.

                         KATIA
               Does not matter! I will date Chris.

                         MAGGIE
               The believer Chris?

INT. PUB. EVENING.

Katia is sitting with Chris at the table. They drink beer.
Chris starts to cry.

                         CHRIS
               And during this pilgrimage I noticed,
               how God is important in my life. I
               also met there my ex-wife...

Katia's phone starts to ring. Katia answers without
hesitation.

                         KATIA
          Yes, I'm on date... How heavy it is?
          OK. I will ask.

                         CHRIS
          Who was it?

                         KATIA
          Can my friends join us? They have
          some problem...

INT. PUB. EVENING.

Anna and Maggie join Katia and Chris. They have party
dresses and look amazing.

                         MAGGIE
          Maybe you could help me? I found this
          cheap TV set, but it is very heavy...

                         CHRIS
          No problem. Let's go!

                         ANNA
          Let's buy some more drinks!

INT. MAGGIE'S HOUSE. LATE EVENING.

Chris is carrying a very old and very heavy TV set up the
stairs. He is struggling, but finally carries it up to
Maggie's room.

                         CHRIS
          Katia, can I leave overnight? I'm too
          drunk to drive.

                         MAGGIE
          I have spare room for guests.

INT. MAGGIE'S HOUSE. MAGGIES'S BEDROOM. LATE EVENING.

It's dark. Maggie is coming back from the bathroom, after
having a shower. She looks tired. She switches of the hall's
lights and enters the bedroom. She sits on her bed and
starts to shout. She jumps and run to switch on the lights.

The light are on. We do not see anything unusal firstly.
Suddenly the quilt moves and uncovers naked Chris body.

                    MAGGIE
     What the hell are you doing here?

                    CHRIS
     I just needed a hug! If you love God
     you should also love me!

INT. CAFE. DAY.

Katia, Anna and Maggie are sitting at the table and
laughing.

                    MAGGIE
     I told him to go away! Nothing really
     happened.

                    KATIA
     He was not my type, I like hiking,
     but pilgrims are out of my league.
     Anyways, I have a new date in half an
     hour.

                    ANNA
     Who is it?

Katia shows them a picture of very handsome man.

                    ANNA (cont'd)
     This is your date? If he will be
     boring, you can call us...

                    KATIA
     I should handle the situation. I've
     even prepared first line, not to get
     stuck.

                    MAGGIE
     What is your first line?

                    KATIA
     It's just simple "How was your
     journey".

They all start to laugh.

                    ANNA
     I wish to have such date...

EXT. NEXT TO THE FOUNTAIN. AFTERNOON.

Katia is walking nervously around the fountain and checking
her phone. Suddenly a man, ALBERT, who could win a Quasimodo
role, very ugly, troll alike, approaches Katia.

                    ALBERT
          Hi, it's me.

                    KATIA
          I think we did not met before...

                    ALBERT
          It's me, your date. I have some old
          pictures on my profile...

                    KATIA
          How was your journey?

                    ALBERT
          What journey?

                    KATIA
          Here... You live quite far...

                    ALBERT
          I have quite fast bike!

INT. PUB. EVENING.

Katia and Albert are sitting next to the bar and drinking
beer.

                    KATIA
          If a history is your hobby...

                    ALBERT
          Yes, especially WWII.

                    KATIA
          Tell me in such case more about
          Lorenzo.

                    ALBERT
          Lorenzo?

                    KATIA
          Yes, there was Enigma and Lorenzo.

                    ALBERT
          I will go to order more drinks. What
          would you like?

Albert is going for drinks. Katia checks her phone, which
starts to ring.

> ANNA
> Are you alive? We are worried. It's
> total stranger!

> KATIA
> Yes, I'm fine. We are just chatting
> about history...

> ANNA
> Listen, can we join you? I feel very
> low tonight!

> KATIA
> Yes, we are in the pub next to the
> corner.

> ANNA
> We can go to circus and the fun fair
> next to it...

INT. PUB. EVENING.

Katia and Albert are chatting, when Katia sees her friends
behind the back of Albert. She waves to them.

Anna and Maggie are giggling till the time Albert turns
around. Their smiles disappears. Their jaws drop.

> ALBERT
> I will go to order more drinks, and
> after that we can go to fun fair.

Albert leaves them. Girls are still in shock.

> ANNA
> Where did you find this creature?

Albert is coming back, carrying the beers.

> ANNA (cont'd)
> So, how do you find your date?

> KATIA
> We have few topics to share
> together...

Albert is staring at Anna and looks delighted.

EXT. NEXT TO SUPERMARKET. LATE EVENING.

Albert and Katia are standing next to the supermarket
entrance.

                    ALBERT
          You have very nice friends! So what's
          the plan?

                    KATIA
          I need to do some shopping.

                    ALBERT
          Same me.

INT. SUPERMARKET. LATE EVENING.

Albert is stopping next to the meat supply and he takes a
big joint out of the self.

                    ALBERT
          How big is your oven?

                    KATIA
          Listen, I'm a vegetarian.

                    ALBERT
          But you could cook it for me?

                    KATIA
          I had nice time, but I prefer to go
          back home alone.

Albert puts away the joint with angry face.

INT. KATIA'S ROOM. DAY.

Katia is sleeping, when her phone starts to ring. She
answers. It's Albert.

                    ALBERT
          Listen, I have crush for Anna. Can
          you give me her phone number?

                    KATIA
          I would need to ask. Give me few
          minutes.

Katia calls Anna.

                         KATIA (cont'd)
          Your wish came through. My date has a
          crush on you.

                         ANNA
          This creature? You must be joking!

                         KATIA
          He wants your phone number.

                         ANNA
          No freaking way! No, no, no, in any
          case no.

Katia calls back Albert.

                         KATIA
          So, she said she can give you an
          email firstly, as she is afraid of
          strangers.

                         ALBERT
          Email is fine. Text it to me.

He ends call without saying goodbye.

                         KATIA
          Oh, you fucking meat eater! We'll
          see!

Katia sends a message to Albert with email address.

Then she rushes to the laptop and opens her email box in the
search tab. Soon e-mail from Albert comes in. "Dear Anna, It
would be nice to meet soon. Albert."

Katia replies: "Come by train, I have some good ideas for
having fun."

Albert replies: "When?"

Katia replies: "Tonight! Let's meet next to the station, but
I finish my shift after 10 P.M. Is it OK?"

Albert replies: "Yeah. Can I stay at yours later?"

Katia replies: "Yes, of course!"

EXT. NEXT TO THE TRAIN STATION. LATE EVENING.

Albert is standing next to the entrance. The railway worker
excuses him.

RAILWAY WORKER
Sorry sir, we are closing the
station.

ALBERT
What? What time was the return train
to Maidstone?

RAILWAY WORKER
About ten minutes ago.

Albert calls Katia.

ALBERT
Your friend... Where is she?

KATIA
I have no idea, have not seen her
today. Why?

ALBERT
Can you give me her phone number?

KATIA
Well...

ALBERT
An some taxi service number! Text
them to me!

Albert is ending call without saying goodbye.

INT. KATIA'S ROOM. EVENING.

Katia is laughing.

KATIA
You fucking meat lover, let's roll.

She is texting two numbers to Albert.

EXT. NEXT TO THE TRAIN STATION. LATE EVENING.

Albert is looking at his phone's screen. The battery show
10% status.

Albert is calling first number.

ALBERT
Anna? Where are you? We supposed to
have some fun...

                    CHRIS
          Anna? Did you mean my ex-wife? What
          fucking fun are you going to have?
          Where are you?

                    ALBERT
          Sorry mate, it's a mistake.

                    CHRIS
          It's not a mistake! Where are you? I
          will fucking show you fun!

Albert hangs out. His battery shows 5% status. Albert
hesitates and chooses the second phone number.

                    ALBERT
          Hi, I got your phone from Katia or
          Anna. How much would be a drive to
          Maidstone?

                    BEN
          Is this a joke? Do you think I am a
          taxi man?

                    ALBERT
          Actually, yes.

                    BEN
          You are wrong, bro. And your mistake
          was to meet those lesbians. Did you
          meet all three of them? Did you pay
          for their drinks?

                    ALBERT
          Fuck!

His phone shuts down.

<u>God's mistake</u>

Written by

Katarzyna Adamus

Draft
information
2

Fade in

EXT. OUTSIDE OF A "DREAMER INN" PUB. EVENING.

Two men, JASON and GREG, barely standing on their feet, are
loudly talking to each other. They wear military alike
clothes.

                    JASON
          I'm telling you, bro, this is my
          mission, this is what I was born to
          do!

                    GREG
          Nonsense! Get your shit together and
          find a job! My uncle...

                    JASON
          I'm telling you! Watch tomorrow
          newspaper's headlines!

                    GREG
          Who's reading nowadays? Everyone is
          watching TV! My other uncle...

                    JASON
          If you want to help me, get me a
          taxi.

Greg takes out a phone. He orders a taxi.

                    GREG
          It won't be long.

                    JASON
          Thank you, man. Maybe this was your
          life mission to make me safe.

Taxi approaches. Jason gets to the car.

                    GREG
          I was born for more important things,
          you lunatic.

Greg spits on the pavement.

INT. INSIDE A TAXI. EVENING.

Jason is talking to NIKUL, the taxi driver. We can spot that
Nikul has Asian origin. He is wearing modern clothes and has
modern haircut.

                    JASON
          Where do you come from? You remind me
          of this shitty prime minister, no
          offense. Are you from Pakistan?

                    NIKUL
          My parents are from India. They are
          Sikhs.

                    JASON
          This bullshit talking! I did not ask
          about your parents! Where are you
          from?

                    NIKUL
          I was born here.

                    JASON
          Do you think you are English? You
          aren't. And you will never be! Never.

Nikul stops the taxi in the middle of nowhere.

                    NIKUL
          I'm afraid this is the end of your
          ride. I will not allow you to offense
          me.

                    JASON
          Your job is to drive! Maybe your
          mission, your purpose of life was to
          drive me today! Nothing more! Because
          you are no one! I will tell you! Your
          life has no purpose because you are
          from somewhere, where there is no
          God. Somewhere, where life is cheap,
          like you. You are God's mistake!

                    NIKUL
          That's enough!

Nikul gets out of the car. He opens the back door, grabs
Jason and with some resistance of the drunk man, manages to
take him out. He pushes him. Jason falls on the road's
shoulder.

EXT. THE ROAD. LATE EVENING.

Jason is barely walking. He falls. He takes out the phone.
He starts to call MATT.

                         JASON
            Sir, there has been some trouble...

                         MATT
            What's going on? Are you pissed?

                         JASON
            I drunk two or something like that...
            There is a problem! I stuck somewhere
            in the middle of nowhere. Our
            tomorrow mission...

                         MATT
            What mission? You are drunk!

                         JASON
            The mission, the one, I can't talk
            about!

                         MATT
            So why are you talking about it? Did
            you lose your fucking mind?

Jason starts to shout.

                         JASON
            You have to help me! It is my
            mission! Mine! You know you can't
            replace me!

                         MATT
            Oh really?

Matt hangs out. Jason starts to hitchhiking, but no one
stops.

INT. INSIDE A TAXI. EVENING.

Nikul is driving very fast. The incoming call's sound makes
him shouting.

                         NIKUL
            Not now! Fuck you all!

The TAXI OPERATOR starts to chase him through the radio.

                         TAXI OPERATOR
            Nikul! Pick up the phone, or everyone
            will hear this! Nikul!

The phone starts to ring again. Nikul answers.

                         NIKUL
          I have a break! I reported it!

                    TAXI OPERATOR
          We had a phone call that you left
          someone in the middle of nowhere!

                         NIKUL
          I was offended! I will not allow
          anyone...

                    TAXI OPERATOR
          Tomorrow is your last day in our
          company. And better show up, or you
          will not find the job anywhere.
          Fucking princess!

Nikul switches off the phone. He pushes the gas pedal and
starts to drive faster.

EXT. THE SMALL TOWN MAIN STREET. DAY.

PRIME MINISTER is giving a speech, surrounded by the crowd.

                    PRIME MINSTER
          ... This was a tough time. We managed
          to overcome all obstacles, with our
          unbeaten spirit. Today your spirit
          might be down, but I am saying you...

Suddenly a bullet hits him in the chest. The Prime minister
falls down. The crowd starts to shout. The panic begins.

INT. HOTEL ROOM. DAY.

Matt, a man in his forties, is hiding a sniper gun. He is
mumbling under his nose.

                         MATT
          How is your spirit now!

He leaves the room.

EXT. TAXI RANK. DAY.

MICHAEL, around 50 years old man, with grey hair, approaches
the last taxi. Outside of the car, Nikul is smoking a
cigarette.

                    MICHAEL
          Are you free?

                    NIKUL
          I have a break! I will be free in ten
          minutes.

                    MICHAEL
          How much time it will take to get
          other taxi?

                    NIKUL
          Twenty five minutes.

                    MICHAEL
          It's quite important...

                    NIKUL
          I am important as well!

                    MICHAEL
          I will pay you well! I need to get to
          the hospital!

Nikul throws the cigarette and gets inside the car.

                    NIKUL
          I am not helping you because I want
          to. I'm helping you, because that's
          how my parents brought me up. To be
          honest, I totally do not care about
          your health issues.

Nikul starts the engine. Michael gets into the taxi. The car
enters the traffic.

INT. INSIDE A TAXI. DAY.

Nikul is driving steady a taxi. Michael looks nervous.

                    MICHAEL
          Are you able to drive fast? Like
          really fast?

                    NIKUL
          I'm not an ambulance. I might lose my
          license.

                    MICHAEL
          I promise, you won't lose it! Just
          tell me if you can drive very well...

                         NIKUL
              I can show you. It is my last day
              anyway.

Nikul speeds up. His car is taking over one by one all cars
on the motorway. He speeds up even more.

EXT. OUTSIDE OF THE HOSPITAL. DAY.

Nikul stops outside of the A&E entry. Michael opens fast the
door and runs into the building.

                         NIKUL
              What the fuck! My money!

He parks the taxi and enters the hospital building.

INT. HOSPITAL RECEPTION. DAY.

Confused Nikul asks RECEPTIONIST.

                         NIKUL
              Have you seen this man? Grey hair?
              Just running inside? He did not
              fucking pay!

                         RECEPTIONIST
              Ah! Michael! He is out best surgeon!
              We had some emergency here. The prime
              minister...

Nikul interrupts.

                         NIKUL
              I'm sick and tired of listening about
              the prime minister. He is not from
              Pakistan, my parents are from India,
              and I am fucking English! I finished
              my MBA just to drive this taxi,
              because you are all racists! Just
              give me my money! I have my bills to
              pay!

Receptionist picks up the phone.

                         THE RECEPTIONIST
              We have some awkward situation.
              Michael did not pay his bill for a
              taxi on his way to the theatre...
              Yes, that's fine. I will cover the
              expenses.

She puts the phone away and takes out her handbag. She gives
100 pounds to Nikul. He looks concerned.

                    NIKUL
          It's 30 pounds only, madam.

                    RECEPTIONIST
          Michael told me about your commitment
          to driving. Please accept the money!

Nikul takes the money and leaves the building.

EXT. OUTSIDE OF THE HOTEL. SWIMMING POOL AREA. DAY.

Matt is sunbathing and drinking an alcoholic drink. Suddenly
his phone rings. Matt checks, who is calling. A nasty
grimace pops out on his face.

                    MATT
          I told you not to call anymore!

                    JASON
          This was my mission! Mine! You
          screwed it! You screwed it
          completely!

                    MATT
          What do you mean?

                    JASON
          He is still fucking alive. And you
          know why? Because this was my
          mission. This was what I was born
          for. You supposed to just serve me on
          my way...

                    MATT
          You are forgetting yourself, I guess!

                    JASON
          This was my mission!

                    MATT
          Maybe you were born just to drink too
          much and annoy people. Piss off!

Matt hangs out. He starts to drink his drink and make a
comfortable position. He continues to sunbath.

EXT. TAXI RANK. DAY.

Nikul is sitting in his taxi. Jason approaches his car from
behind and gets inside.

INT. INSIDE A TAXI. DAY.

                    JASON
          Drive! Fast! To the hospital!

Nikul turns around. He starts to shout.

                    NIKUL
          Get out of my car!

                    JASON
          I knew we will meet again.

Jason takes out the gun and points it at Nikul.

                    JASON (cont'd)
          Drive, you fucking bin Laden.

Nikul starts the engine and he enters the traffic.

                    JASON (cont'd)
          I will tell you something! Everyone
          in this world has a mission to
          fulfill. And he can only die, after
          he completed it. And you, you are a
          God's mistake. Did I tell you this?
          Your mission is to serve my mission.
          Drive faster!

Nikul starts to drive faster.

EXT. OUTSIDE OF THE HOSPITAL. DAY.

Jason gets out of the car and shoots Nikul. Then he enters
the building.

INT. HOSPITAL RECEPTION. DAY.

Jason, with his gun hidden, approaches Receptionist.

                    JASON
          Good afternoon. I am the reporter
          from a local newspaper. Is there a
          chance to visit the prime minister?

                    RECEPTIONIST
Oh! You are late!

                    JASON
What do you mean? Did he die?

                    RECEPTIONIST
No. Our best surgeon, Michael, has
done a proper job. Prime minister is
secure now, on his way to the royal
hospital.

                    JASON
Ah! I see. Thank you, darling.

EXT. OUTSIDE OF THE HOSPITAL. DAY.

Jason takes out the body of the Nikul from the car. He puts
it in a sitting position on the bus stop bench. Then he gets
to the car.

INT. INSIDE A TAXI. DAY.

Jason is murmuring to himself.

                    JASON
I will make it! I will make it one
day!

He starts an engine and leaves the hospital area.

Fade out

Matchmakers

Written by

Katarzyna Adamus

Fade in

INT. ARTHUR'S ROOM. EVENING.

The room design is very simple. One single bed, wardrobe,
and desk. On the wall cross and the picture of Saint Mary
with Jesus as a baby. At the desk is sitting ARTHUR, a young
blond man, quite handsome but wearing traditional office
clothes and haircut. He is studying the Bible. Suddenly we
hear loud knocking to the door and the housemate MARK gets
into the room. He is dressed in a cool way and looks like
the opposite of Arthur. Mark is carrying a few beers and is
whistling a popular song under his nose.

                    ARTHUR
          I did not say you can enter!

                    MARK
          I know you are not jerking at all, so
          what is this fuss about? Listen, we
          have something to celebrate!

                    ARTHUR
          We, or you? I'm praying at the
          moment!

                    MARK
          Listen, do not try to be more saint
          than Jesus. Peter will not let you in
          to paradise. You know, in this rat
          race you would be a competition...

Arthur closes the Bible. He looks at Mark with contempt.

                    ARTHUR
          So what are you going to celebrate?

Mark is taking out from the pocket a paper. He unfolds it
and shows it to Arthur.

                    ARTHUR (cont'd)
          So you paid for another certificate?

                    MARK
          What do you mean?

                    ARTHUR
          These awards... You said you were
          paying something towards it?

                    MARK
          I paid the entry fee, it's obvious!

                        ARTHUR
              Greg was right.

Mark sits at the bed. He folds his arms and starts to stare
at the floor.

                        MARK
              Tell me about it.

                        ARTHUR
              So you admit it?

                        MARK

              Admit what?

                        ARTHUR
              That you paid to someone to design
              all these laurels and certificates...

Mark gets up and is going to the doors. He leaves.

INT. MARK'S ROOM. EVENING.

Mark's room is in chaos. Between the piles of books and
clothes, there is not even a path to the desk and the bed.
There are just few places to put the feet and jump over
them. Mark knows where to put the feet perfectly. He did not
clean up for last the two months. On the walls, we see
screenwriting awards certificates. Mark switches on the
laptop and puts on some western music. He opens the beer and
stares with empty eyes through the window.

Sudden, loud knocking to the doors. Arthur enters the room
and falls over the vacuum cleaner arm.

                        ARTHUR
              Jesus Christ! What have you been
              doing here!

                        MARK
              Paying for my awards.

                        ARTHUR
              Listen, if it's so easy to get them,
              I will make myself rich soon.

                        MARK
              Good luck.

                    ARTHUR
          I have even an idea already. Imagine
          that sheep is a cursed princess and
          the prince of a different state is
          going to sacrifice her to...

Mark starts to laugh.

                    ARTHUR (cont'd)
          I won't tell you more, because you
          could steal my idea.

EXT. LONDON STREET. DAY.

It's a rainy autumn day. People pass each other, without
making eye contact. Suddenly one of them turns around, to
change direction. It's Mark. He bumps into Arthur.

                    MARK
          Long time!

                    ARTHUR
          Yes, two years exactly! You should
          ask me!

                    MARK
          Pardon?

                    ARTHUR
          You should ask, how is my writing!

                    MARK
          Are you kidding me?

                    ARTHUR
          I just completed the script and I am
          meeting the literary agent today. I
          wrote to him that it is his life
          chance and he seemed to be
          interested.

                    MARK
          A sheep script?

                    ARTHUR
          I added some Christian subtext to it.

                    MARK
          Oh my fucking God...

                              ARTHUR
          And Maggie, you know, the one who
          wrote your scripts...

                              MARK
          Maggie just put two commas and
          changed the form of one verb, to be
          honest...

                              ARTHUR
          ...So she said it is brilliant. By
          the way, do you have her phone
          number? I lost contact with her few
          moths ago, she moved somewhere...

Mark takes out a pen and paper and writes down the number
from his phone. He hands it to Arthur.

                              MARK
          You two would be a good couple
          together, honestly.

                              ARTHUR
          Shut up! Now listen, I have to go, I
          have a meeting with this literary
          manager. Wait for me somewhere, this
          will be worthy of celebration!

INT. ENGLISH PUB. AFTERNOON.

Mark is drinking a beer at one of the tables. He watches the
football match on the pub's TV screen. His phone rings. We
just see the numbers. Mark seems to be intrigued. He answers
the phone.

                              ARTHUR
          Where are you? I have really good
          news!

INT. ENGLISH PUB. AFTERNOON.

Mark is looking with his eyes wide open at Arthur. Arthur is
very loud. There are many empty glasses on their table.

                              MARK
          And then?

                              ARTHUR
          Then he said something critical to
          the plot.

                    MARK
          What did he say?

Arthur lowers his voice tone.

                    ARTHUR
          He asked... He asked why not a cow
          instead of the sheep!

Mark starts to laugh and he can't stop. After a while, he
tries to say something, but he can't. With few more
attempts, he says:

                    MARK
          Listen, man! It's a waste of time! He
          had definitely fun at your cost!

                    ARTHUR
          Do you have a literary manager?

                    MARK
          Not yet, but...

                    ARTHUR
          You are just jealous!

                    MARK
          It's time for me!

                    ARTHUR
          You gave me the wrong number to
          Maggie by the way.

                    MARK
          She could change her number.

                    ARTHUR
          Yeah, sure. And remember, the sheep
          idea is copyrighted.

                    MARK
          But cow's idea not yet.

Mark leaves the pub laughing. Arthur looks at him with wide
open mouth. He grabs the phone and calls.

                    ARTHUR
          Hi, I just would like to know, if I
          can copyright the script idea over
          the phone?

INT. COFFEE SHOP IN LONDON. DAY.

Mark is drinking coffee and writing on his laptop. He sits
next to the window. He looks from time to time at the
passing by people. One of the females, dressed in a long
brown coat and grey cap starts to wave to him. She enters
the coffee shop. It's Maggie. She is young and walks with
confidence. She approaches Mark.

                    MAGGIE
          Still living a dream?

                    MARK
          It's a job now, I do not complain.

                    MAGGIE
          What kind of job? Did you finally
          listened to me and you are now the
          accountant?

                    MARK
          Listen, I met Arthur few weeks ago.
          You are enough sensible to handle
          him. I will give you his phone
          number.

EXT. PARK IN LONDON. DAY.

Arthur and Maggie are sitting on the bench. There is a big
space between them.

                    ARTHUR
          I'm telling you, he will steal my
          idea!

                    MAGGIE
          Can you write it fast?

                    ARTHUR
          With sheep, I could add some
          Christian context. With cows, only
          Indian one. I started to do some
          research, but it will take some time.

                    MAGGIE
          He is a bad writer, he will not come
          up with any good idea. Last time he
          told me he gets his best ideas in
          this pub next to the...

                    ARTHUR
          It's getting cold. Let's go there.

INT. ENGLISH PUB NUMBER 2. EVENING.

Arthur and Maggie are sitting at the table. They look out of
the place.

                    ARTHUR
          It's just a pub. A pub full of drunk
          lunatics.

One of the pub clients hear this and approaches a couple.
It's OLEG. He's middle aged, medium height and looks like
from everywhere.

                    OLEG
          I misheard your chat. In old years,
          when I was serving my years in KBG,
          my sight and my hearing were totally
          fine...

                    MAGGIE
          We are not interested in your medical
          problems.

                    ARTHUR
          Or your corporation rat's story.

                    OLEG
          I'm not talking about the well known
          London company. I'm talking about
          security services in Russia...

                    ARTHUR
          With my screenwriter's ear, I can
          hear a lie from far distance.

                    OLEG
          A screenwriter? We can make a
          business. I can tell you my story,
          and you write it, then we will share
          the profits!

Arthur tries to ignore him and starts to talk to Maggie.

                    ARTHUR
          So I visited the literary manager and
          he gave me another clue!

                    MAGGIE
          What was it?

ARTHUR
He asked, why it is a princess
instead of the prince! This can
change a lot!

OLEG
Probably the whole story.

Oleg loses his interest. He goes to the bar and orders
another beer.

ARTHUR
You helped Mark to write his
scripts.could you help me as well? I
will give you 10% of profits!

MAGGIE
It's my turn to buy beers.

ARTHUR
You are the first Polish woman, who
offered me a drink! You are amazing!

Maggie goes to the bar and stands next to Oleg.

OLEG
So you are Polish? I was working on
the Polish border too...

MAGGIE
How is it possible? You just said you
were Russian!

OLEG
You would look nice in blond hair
colour...

Maggie orders drinks and comes back to the table.

ARTHUR
What did he say?

MAGGIE
He wanted me to dye my hair into
blond!

ARTHUR
Let's call Mark. I'm sure he wants to
stab my back.

Arthur takes out the phone and calls Mark.

                    ARTHUR (cont'd)
          Hi, it's me.

                    MARK
          The most popular name over the phone!

                    ARTHUR
          I would feel insulted but my name is
          rare. Listen, we have some situation
          here with this KMPG worker from
          Russia. He said he has an interesting
          story ...

                    MARK
          Where are you?

INT. ENGLISH PUB NUMBER 2. LATE EVENING.

Mark enters the pub. He goes to Arthur's and Maggie's table.

                    MARK
          So, where is this accountant?

                    MAGGIE
          I'm happy that you listened to my
          advice. You will be a good
          accountant.

                    MARK
          So where is he?

                    ARTHUR
          We will tell you if you will write
          down here, and sign the paper, that
          you are not going to write a script
          about the cow...

                    MARK
          I swear I won't do that! Neither
          about the sheep!

                    ARTHUR
          Sign the paper!

They prepare the paper which Mark signs quickly. Arthur
points at Oleg. Mark leaves them and joints Oleg at the bar.
He hands him his business card.

                    OLEG
          These two told you about me?

                         MARK
          Don't worry, they do not know what is
          going on.

                         OLEG
          I'm worried about the IQ of their
          kids!

Arthur and Maggie are watching them from the table.

                         MAGGIE
          Pathetic! All this rat race!

                         ARTHUR
          Listen! Listen to this! What if the
          prince is a rat? This would be...

                         MAGGIE
          ... a great story!

They hug each other. Then they split, ashamed. Then they hug
again and start to kiss.

Fade out

Melancholy

Written by

Katarzyna Adamus

Fade in

INT. KITCHEN OF NADIA. LATE EVENING.

NADIA, 40 years old woman, wearing glasses, dressed in a
very elegant female suit is sitting at the kitchen table.
She is staring at OLIVIA, 35 years - old blonde sex-bomb,
wearing a simple tracksuit. Olivia is washing the dishes. On
the table laying bouquet, two glasses, and four bottles of
white wine. The Nadia's glass is full, Olivia's is empty and
untouched.

                    OLIVIA
          Yeah, yeah... OK. You know? I think
          you overestimate it all.

                    NADIA
          What do you mean?

                    OLIVIA
          You are the professor, you should
          know what I mean! You overestimate
          this title. Did it give you more
          money?

                    NADIA
          I thought we will be celebrating! I'm
          not ready to be bullied by my best
          friend!

                    OLIVIA
          I never said I'm your best friend.
          But if you think that I am, listen to
          me - do you want to die in the
          library?

                    NADIA
          People are second to books for me.

                    OLIVIA
          That's why you should not have a
          professor title. You don't know life
          at all. When did you have sex last
          time?

Nadia starts to drink wine.

                    NADIA
          You would not believe me.

Olivia stops washing the dishes. She goes to the table,
pours the wine to her glass, and starts to drink as well.

                         OLIVIA
          I do not believe because you
          overestimate things. Like with this
          celebration. Professor! Pathetic.

                         NADIA
          I had sex yesterday.

                         OLIVIA
          How is it possible? Who was it? You
          know... Men has to like a woman to do
          this if you know what I mean. I'm
          sure you lie!

Nadia chokes with the wine.

                         NADIA
          OK, you think I am ugly, know my
          opinion about you - you are cold like
          fish! When did you last time sleep
          with your boyfriend?

                         OLIVIA
          Why are you asking about my sexual
          life? Do you have some wild fantasies
          about me?

                         NADIA
          Yeah, few, criminal kind of nature.
          In case, you did not understand, I'm
          joking.

                         OLIVIA
          First of all, you are a liar. You
          wrote your topic on depression topic,
          right? What do you know exactly about
          it?

Nadia finishes her wine and pours some more.

                         NADIA
          You know what? I have my limits as
          well. Not many people know this.

                         OLIVIA
          Your thesis is shit. For example, I
          like to be depressed.

                         NADIA
          Do not mistake depression for
          melancholy.

                    OLIVIA
          Oh my god. We live in modern times.
          Who uses now such vocabulary.

                    NADIA
          I slept with your boyfriend. If you
          like to feel sad, this will add some
          extra dimension to it.

                    OLIVIA
          I do not believe you.

                    NADIA
          Yes, I was joking.

                    OLIVIA
          He has some standards, you know.

                    NADIA
          Let's talk about your fall for
          sadness. Does the lack of power and
          will to live makes you happy?

                    OLIVIA
          Maybe?!

                    NADIA
          It's melancholy. The fall season is
          coming. The summer past in a fraction
          of time, nothing happened, nothing
          was sorted out. Unconsciously you
          feel your life will never change. You
          start thinking about these few grey
          hairs. About these few wrinkles on
          your forehead.

Olivia jumps out of the chair.

                    OLIVIA
          What wrinkles?

Olivia runs to the bathroom. She comes back with a small
desk mirror.

                    OLIVIA (cont'd)
          Where do you see these wrinkles?
          Maybe on your face!

                    NADIA
          They got deeper each day, with each
          bitter breath you take, with each
          grumpy face you do towards shop
          assistants...

Olivia starts to stare in silence at Nadia.

                    OLIVIA
          You know? Maybe you were right?
          Nothing will change. It's me who
          should get this title, not you.

                    NADIA
          Here it goes.

                    OLIVIA
          But we can fix things, right?

Nadia stares at her. She looks shocked.

                    NADIA
          You did not complete your thesis on
          time! What did you expect?

                    OLIVIA
          You can finish it for me. You can say
          you do not need this title or ob
          post. You do not like students. You
          could be happy as the librarian.

                    NADIA
          I did not suspect you have a sense of
          humour.

                    OLIVIA
          You know what? I feel like in danger.
          You came to my house, you argue with
          me, you slept with my boyfriend and
          now threatening me to finish with
          him...

                    NADIA
          Did you overdose codeine?

Olivia grabs the knife from the washed cutlery.

                    NADIA (cont'd)
          Are you OK?

Olivia slowly starts to approach Nadia with the knife. Nadia
jumps out of the chair.

                    OLIVIA
          Nietzsche was right. Some people are
          lower than others.

Olivia makes attempt to hit Nadia with the knife. Nadia makes a block, she grabs the forearm of Olivia, turns it around, and makes pressure twist on her wrist. The knife falls out of Olivia hand. Nadia grabs it. She pushes away Olivia. Olivia slowly gets out of the floor.

                    OLIVIA (cont'd)
          What the hell. Where did you learn
          this! You fucking motherfucker.

                    NADIA
          Am I overestimating things, or you
          just wanted to kill me?

                    OLIVIA
          You piss me off. You come here with
          your cheap wine...

                    NADIA
          Dry wine is more expensive than this
          sweet shit you are drinking.

The door opens. MARK, Olivia's boyfriend enters the flat.

                    OLIVIA
          Help!

                    NADIA
          Would you be sad after my death?

                    OLIVIA
          Are you joking? You are nothing!
          Help!

Mark gets into the kitchen. He watches two women, concerned.

                    NADIA
          I was just leaving.

                    MARK
          What's going on? There is still wine
          on the table, why you are going?

                    OLIVIA
          I was shouting for help, did not you
          hear?

                    MARK
          Please stop with this codeine.

Nadia puts the knife to her handbag and goes towards the corridor. She puts on her shoes.

Olivia follows her.

                    NADIA
          You were right. I'm too stupid to
          have this professor title. I did not
          see this coming. I thought we are
          friends.

                    OLIVIA
          We are colleagues and we are rivals.
          You should make some therapy
          probably.

                    NADIA
          I will resign from this new post.

Olivia sighs.

                    OLIVIA
          Will you?

                    NADIA
          I like to see you happy...

                    OLIVIA
          I always knew you are kind of
          lesbian.

                    NADIA
          So I will make you sad for a long
          time. Because I was joking about my
          resignation. But you like to be sad?

Olivia runs to the kitchen and grabs the bottle of wine. She
comes back to the corridor and throws it at the place, where
Nadia was standing. But Nadia managed to leave, and the
bottle hits the closing door.

Mark approaches Olivia and hugs her. Olivia bursts in tears.

                    MARK
          They say male friendship is tough,
          but the friendship of two female
          scientists is the most sophisticated
          thing I have ever seen.

Fade out

Name of success

Written by

Katarzyna Adamus

Draft
information
2

Fade in

INT. CONFERENCE HALL. DAY.

The big conference hall is packed with around 1000
attendees. They are standing, clapping their hands and
shouting. On the scene bald, tall, muscular PETER is
shouting to the microphone.

                    PETER
          What's the name of success?

                    CROWD
          Money!!!

                    PETER
          I don't hear you... What's the name
          of success?

                    CROWD
          Money! Money! Money!

                    PETER
          Yes! And let me tell you one more
          thing! It feels soooo goood!

All attendees shout even more and continue to give a
standing ovation.

INT. CORRIDOR NEXT TO THE CONFERENCE HALL. DAY.

Peter is standing next to his poster. Some of the attendees
pay for the ticket to Peter's EMPLOYEE to be able to take a
picture with Peter.

ATTENDEE 1 sneaks and takes a selfie with his face and Peter
in the background. Peter notices this.

                    PETER
          Hey, delete this photo!

                    ATTENDEE 1
          I just took my chance! You were just
          talking about it!

                    PETER
          You got it wrong. If you want to have
          a chance, grab a ticket or pay for my
          course.

Attendee 1 leaves the hall, looking upset.

INT. PETER'S HOUSE. DAY. A FEW MONTHS LATER.

Peter sits on the couch. On the floor piles of unopened
letters with red titles "Open" and "Important mail". Peter
keeps his head in the palms. He grabs suddenly the phone.

> PETER
> Hi! Can you please do me a favor?

> EMPLOYEE
> Sorry. I'm not a charity. You were a
> good teacher. I'm not going to
> surround myself with the bankrupts,
> but with successful people. Law of
> attraction! You must have a shitty
> mind, if you ended up like this.

> PETER
> Listen, I have only three minutes of
> credit left on the phone. Could
> you...

> EMPLOYEE
> Then use it wisely!

The Employee hangs up. Peter dials another number.

> PETER
> Hi! It's me! Could you please give me
> a call back? It's quite important.

> FRIEND 1
> Call me when you will top up your
> credit.

Peter hangs out. He dials the last number.

> PETER
> Mum? Please call me back when you
> hear this message.

Peter hangs out. He takes all the envelopes and puts them to
the fireplace. He sets the fire and watches it.

> PETER (cont'd)
> Money is the name of success! I will
> be rich again! I will be rich again.
> By the end of July, I will earn one
> million dollars. I will be rich
> again!

INT. PETER'S MUM HOUSE. KITCHEN. DAY.

PETER'S MUM is cooking risotto with mushrooms. Peter is
sitting at the table.

                    PETER
          Mum! I am not going to listen to your
          advice. Have you ever earn more than
          a few thousand dollars?

                    PETER'S MUM
          Okey. So call your coach.

                    PETER
          Yes, I will listen to this advice.
          Can I borrow your phone for a while?

EXT. THE GARDEN. DAY.

Peter is nervously smoking a cigarette. He grabs the phone
and dials the number.

                    PETER
          Hi. It's me. I am away from the city.

                    COACH
          Good to hear you! Any good news?

                    PETER
          I don't have good news. I'm bankrupt
          and I sleep on my mum's couch.

                    COACH
          How did it come! You did not listen
          to me at all! Did you do what I told
          you to do? You are such a waste of
          time!

                    PETER
          It was all good, till the time the
          chaos begun. Then it all went
          wrong...

                    COACH
          Listen! I'm not a charity. I will
          send you an invoice for the last few
          coaching hours. And you'd better pay!

                    PETER
          Fuck you! Fuck you!

Coach hangs out. Peter wants to throw the phone but looks at
it and restrains.

                         PETER (cont'd)
              I will be rich again! I will be rich
              again! By the end of August, I will
              earn one hundred thousand dollars! I
              will be rich again!

                         PETER'S MUM (O.S.)
              Dinner is ready!

INT. CONFERENCE HALL. DAY.

The conference hall is full again. Peter is shouting at the
scene.

                         PETER
              I will be rich again! I will be rich
              again!

INT. PETER'S MUM HOUSE. NIGHT.

Peter pops out from the couch. It was only a dream.

INT. PETER'S MUM HOUSE. KITCHEN. DAY.

Peter's Mum is cooking spaghetti. Peter is sitting at the
table.

                         PETER
              Okey. You won. What was this job
              offer about?

EXT. BUSY ROAD. DAY.

Peter is in the mobile restaurant van, frying pancakes.
People are queuing to order them. It looks like a busy
place.

INT. MOBILE RESTAURANT VAN. EVENING.

Peter is whispering to himself. There is no queue anymore.

                         PETER
              I will be rich again. Fuck you, God!

A HOMELESS MAN appears out of nowhere. He stops next to the
restaurant van and stares at the pancakes.

> PETER (cont'd)
> Would you like some? I'm closing and
> don't like to throw away the food.

> HOMELESS MAN
> No, thanks man. I am watching my
> diet. It looks really shitty.

The Homeless Man walks away.

INT. PETER'S MUM HOUSE. KITCHEN. DAY.

Peter and his Mum are eating pancakes.

> PETER
> ...and then he said he wants to stay
> fit...

> PETER'S MUM
> You will never make friends. He might
> be homeless, but he still kept his
> pride. What happened to yours?

> PETER
> There are no friends anymore. Do you
> remember Jake, my old school-fellow?
> I invited him to dinner tomorrow. I
> will show you a real friendship.

INT. PETER'S MUM HOUSE. KITCHEN. DAY.

JAKE, Peter, and Peter's mum are sitting at the table. In
the middle of the table, there is a note saying "new job"
and the phone number.

Jake and Peter are drinking beer.

> JAKE
> We can call it a reunion. I haven't
> seen you for a few years.

> PETER
> Whom are you texting now?

> JAKE
> She's just a friend, you know...

                         PETER
              How is Kelly?

                         JAKE
              We are not getting on well. We are
              separated. If I knew... Maybe you two
              were really meant for each other...

                         PETER
              Nevermind, it is an old story. We
              liked her both, she has chosen you.
              The reality of a small town.

Jake hides his phone, on which he was texting someone. The
phone starts to ring in Peter's pocket. He takes out the
brand new phone.

                         PETER'S MUM
              Did you buy a new phone?

Peter takes his beer and pours it over Jake's head.

                         PETER
              Get the hell out of here. And I don't
              want to see you for the next few
              months!

Jake grabs his jacket and leaves the house angry.

                         PETER'S MUM
              What was it all about?

                         PETER
              Nevermind.

                         PETER'S MUM
              Give me your new phone number. I'm
              worried about you. You behave
              strangely recently.

                         PETER
              It's on this note.

He grabs the note with a "new job" title and hands to his
mum.

EXT. MOBILE RESTAURANT VAN. EVENING.

Few HOMELESS MEN are standing next to the van and listening
to Peter. All of them are eating pancakes.

                    PETER
          Listen to this! The law of attraction
          works! All mantras work! Repeat after
          me: "I will be rich again!"

                    HOMELESS MAN
          Man, what's wrong with you? I was
          never rich. Did you?

Peter thinks for a while then answers.

                    PETER
          No, probably not.

Homeless Men start to whisper.

                    HOMELESS MEN
          We will be rich! By the end of
          September, we will earn ten thousand
          dollars. We will be rich!

                    HOMELESS MAN
          And happy! Oh yes!

                    HOMELESS MEN
          Amen!

Fade out

<u>Promotion</u>

Written by

Katarzyna Adamus

Draft
information
2

Fade in

EXT. POPLARS' ALLEY. DAY.

ANTHONY (middle-aged man in glasses, wearing black suit
trousers and jumper with diamonds pattern) is walking down
the alley with MARGARET (middle-aged woman in pink dress),
who holds a rose in her hand.

                    ANTHONY
          No, I don't date often. How about
          you?

                    MARGARET
          It is my first date since the
          divorce, my husband was a total
          asshole, he...

Anthony takes her hand and interrupts.

                    ANTHONY
          All the leaves have fallen. Do you
          feel the smell?

                    MARGARET
          Yes, this smell and whole weather are
          telling me, that I should be inside a
          cozy room, with a warm blanket... If
          you know what I mean.

                    ANTHONY
          Ah yes! And with the book!

Margaret takes back her hand.

                    ANTHONY (cont'd)
          Sorry! I do not feel the smell. At
          this season I got inflammation of my
          sinuses. And in the summer is even
          worse, I got hay fever. I have also
          astigmatism! I see everything like on
          impressionism pictures!

                    MARGARET
          So, what is your job?

                    ANTHONY
          I'm an archivist. I work with papers
          in the city council.

                         MARGARET
         How boring! On the last date I met a
         lawyer! He was traveling a lot!

                         ANTHONY
         Last date? I thought I am your first
         date?

                         MARGARET
         No, actually not. I had also a date
         with a banker.

                         ANTHONY
         And what is your job?

                         MARGARET
         I was full-time mum. Now...

                         ANTHONY
         Now you are looking for a rich
         boyfriend, am I correct?

Margaret hands the rose to Anthony.

                         MARGARET
         I think we are not getting on well.

She turns around, and goes back up the alley, leaving
Anthony with the rose.

INT. ANTHONY'S FLAT. DAY.

Anthony enters the flat. He adds the rose to a few other
roses, situated in the jar on the kitchen table. The dog,
named Professor, appears from the room. Anthony takes out a
dog treat from the shelf and keeps it in his hand.

                         ANTHONY
         Who's the good dog? Who's the good
         dog?

Professor starts to bark. Anthony hands to the dog a treat.

                         ANTHONY (cont'd)
         We need to get this promotion,
         Professor. We are not doing well with
         women.

The dog stops to eat and starts to bark.

                    ANTHONY (cont'd)
          Ah, yes! My Chinese lesson! Thank you
          for reminding me.

INT. ANTHONY'S FLAT. DAY.

We hear knocking at the door. Anthony opens the door, with a
Chinese textbook in his hand, and sees his NEIGHBOUR (30
years old man).

                    NEIGHBOUR
          I thought you were learning French!

                    ANTHONY
          I learn French in the morning.

                    NEIGHBOUR
          You are so, so smart. Can you do me a
          favour?

                    ANTHONY
          Your favour costs the same as a
          monthly promotion!

                    NEIGHBOUR
          Just a fiver, please. And if you ever
          would need some prints, I can do this
          for you. I have access to the
          machines. I heard you want to write a
          book, I could print some copies.

Anthony hands him the money and the Neighbour goes back to
his flat.

                    ANTHONY
          I would probably have all library
          full till this time.

INT. ANTHONY'S OFFICE. DAY.

We see three very busy working women: ALICE (30), BARBARA
(40) and JULIA (50), and one young man, TEO (27), who looks
like a supermodel. Anthony pretends that he is working on
some data. On the desks lots of personal items - family
pictures, cosmetics etc.

                    ANTHONY (V.O.)
          "Promotions, promotions!" - I hear
          this word several hundred times a
          day.
                         (MORE)

                    ANTHONY (V.O.) (cont'd)
          Everybody's gone crazy! They have
          stopped surfing the Internet and
          pretend to be faithful employees.

We see all employees in the office, working hard on some
papers and using computers, printing machines.

                    ANTHONY (V.O.) (cont'd)

           Only gossip can't stop. All the
           staff in the department are women,
           except for the administrator, who
           would do better working as a
           supermodel. He would have made more
           money, and the situation in the
           department would have improved if the
           clerks hadn't been running every five
           minutes to his desk under the pretext
           of doing some very important
           business.

We see Alice, taking her papers and going to the desk of
Teo, and asking some questions and pointing on the paper.

                    ANTHONY (V.O.) (cont'd)

           Coming back to the rumors, I know
           everything about their neighbours,
           their marital, extramarital and
           premarital lives. Everything is a bit
           distorted by the point of view of the
           interested parties, so it is
           difficult to say what is objective
           truth in these relations. Anyway,
           does the objective truth exist? There
           are objective facts, but if they
           concern several different people,
           then their way of perceiving events
           is different because of their
           character, experience, etc. The truth
           is that if they concern several
           different people, then their way of
           perceiving events is different.

Julia comes to the desk of Anthony with a big pile of
documents. She has a malicious smile, when she puts it on
his desk.

                    ANTHONY
          What is it?

JULIA
Someone needs to put numbers on the
corners of the pages. With a pen.

ANTHONY
I thought it is your job?

Julia leans towards Anthony and whispers to his ear.

JULIA
When I get this promotion, I will be
your boss. So be nice!

Anthony takes the big pile and starts to put the numbers in
the corners, one page by one. The pile is really big.
Anthony looks at the pile and then at all workers.

ANTHONY (V.O.)
To get a promotion, you have to be
better than others or try not to let
other people get it - then it will
come to us. But how to sabotage the
work of other clerks?

INT. ANTHONY'S OFFICE. DAY.

Anthony pretends being very busy. On his desk many travel
magazines and trips fliers. It is quite a big pile of
brochures. Julia comes to the desk of Anthony. She takes all
pile of travel brochures.

JULIA
You don't need it right now, do you?

ANTHONY
Help yourself.

Julia takes brochures with her and comes back to her desk.
Soon Alice and Barbara are gathering next to her. They scan
the brochures and chat.

JULIA
I always wanted to go to Africa, but
I was afraid someone will kidnap me
and will make his wife.

ALICE
I thought you are married?

JULIA
I'm still attractive, so no one would
care.

> BARBARA
> Malta is close to Africa. It is very
> warm there for the whole year.

> ALICE
> Look at this! So cheap! And it is
> Venice!

> JULIA
> You don't have a partner to go. I
> will ask my husband about his
> holidays' dates. We must go!

EXT. POPLARS' ALLEY. DAY.

Anthony walks with the dog, Professor. It is raining and
getting dark.

Anthony is talking to the dog while walking.

> ANTHONY
> Professor, our last idea was
> brilliant. Clerks who had partners
> started to think about how to get
> their partners to finance their
> travel and get a holiday at the same
> time. The singles studied romantic
> photos of Venice, dreaming that they
> would meet their dream partner on the
> road. Holiday romances! What is the
> purpose and charm of this? Come to
> bed with a newly met person, and
> after a few days to split. A
> substitute for a relationship. They
> will probably come back blooming
> after such an adventure, their desire
> for acceptance will be satisfied. But
> they will still be lonely. It's
> better to get to know someone well on
> the Internet.

The dog starts to bark.

> ANTHONY (cont'd)
> Yes, I think it is another good idea.

INT. ANTHONY'S OFFICE. DAY.

This time all desk of the office workers are tidy and look
empty, comparing to the past. Also, the clothes are more
modest now.

                        ANTHONY (V.O.)
            I am irritated by their sudden, fake
            enthusiasm. All personal belongings
            and disorder have disappeared from
            the desks. Every other person bought
            various organizers for files, office
            supplies, and incoming documents.
            Cheeky blouses were replaced by
            subdued colors. There is nothing more
            to see. Everything is covered up. The
            skirts have been extended by a good
            twenty centimetres. Such is the power
            of promotion!

On the desk of Anthony this time is laying a pile of
brochures about Internet dating.

Julia comes with a big pile of documents.

                        JULIA
            Other documents need some numbers.
            Try this time to write more
            carefully. We could not decipher most
            of your numbers last time.

Julia spots the brochures.

                        JULIA (cont'd)
            Oh my God! Alice, Barbara, I've got
            something for you!

She takes the brochures and says to Anthony.

                        JULIA (cont'd)
            You don't need it, do you?

INT. ANTHONY'S OFFICE. DAY.

All workers are watching fliers and surfing the Internet.

                        ANTHONY (V.O.)
            I used to drop off the nets for a
            week, bringing in leaflets from
            travel agencies and printouts about
            online romances in alternation. I
            have to boast of a small success. One
            of the most successful female
            employees to be promoted, Julia, has
            already planned her vacation. She
            chose Malta because of the low price
            of the trip and the size of the
            country.
                        (MORE)

ANTHONY (V.O.) (cont'd)
Other workers are surfing the
Internet and chatting on online
dating sites. Really good news!

INT. STAIRCASE. DAY.

Anthony is knocking to the doors of his Neighbour. After a
while, the door opens and the Neighbour goes out.

                    ANTHONY
          Can I ask you for another favour?
          This time I will need some design
          work as well...

INT. ANTHONY'S OFFICE. DAY.

On the desk of Anthony there are laying new leaflets about
TV sets promotion.

Everyone pretends busy work.

                    ANTHONY (V.O.)
          The leaflets are ready. Wouldn't
          anyone be tempted to buy a TV set at
          a third of the supermarket price? And
          I know they are watching TV. I have
          chosen the campaign hours for the
          period when our manager most often
          appears at work. He probably sleeps
          until ten o'clock because he lives
          next door to the office, and he shows
          up half an hour later. The date and
          time are probably the same as the
          date and time of promotion results.
          The campaign will last for only half
          an hour, which is supposed to explain
          the low price of television sets. I
          informed in advertising materials
          that there will be only ten TV sets
          at this price. But for what they are!
          Awesome, so that a whole year's bonus
          from promotion wouldn't be enough for
          them. We will see what my colleagues
          will choose and what they will do
          with their work. I am excited about
          my prank. From time to time I imagine
          the possible consequences of my
          action. But you live only once.

Julia approaches with a big pile of documents. She takes the
leaflets, this time without asking.

                    ANTHONY (V.O.) (cont'd)
          Yes, you all deserve this!

INT. ANTHONY'S OFFICE. DAY.

All workers pretend to work, but they nervously check the
time.

                    ANTHONY (V.O.)
          Today is the day of announcing who is
          the chosen one. The time of the TV
          campaign is approaching. Employees
          nervously pick their nails. The
          tension is more intense than in
          electric cables.

Anthony gets up, takes a packet of cigarettes, and is
preparing to go out.

                    JULIA
          Where are you going?

                    ANTHONY
          Just for a fag!

                    JULIA
          We are going all for a fag now! You
          must stay here, we can't go all at
          the same time.

                    ANTHONY
          I did not know that you all smoke?
          Since when?

                    ALICE
          Does an old bachelor can know
          something about life or women?

Everyone starts to laugh. Anthony sits back. Other workers
put on their clothes in a hurry.

                    JULIA
          Hurry up! They got only ten items!

All workers leave, except Anthony.

INT. ANTHONY'S OFFICE. DAY.

The MANAGER (40) enters the office. He is wearing an elegant
suit. He looks around, confused.

                              MANAGER
                    I wanted to call a meeting... But I
                    can see that there is no one here...

                              ANTHONY
                    If there's no one here, who are you
                    talking to?

The manager clears his throat and gives Anthony "the look".

                              MANAGER
                    So where did our friends go?

                              ANTHONY
                    The TV sets were given away for 20
                    pounds each, but only ten items.

                              MANAGER
                    Well, that's right. I'll take a walk
                    there. Someone has to save our dear
                    girls from the hustle and bustle of
                    shopping, right? But what can you
                    know about it!

Anthony starts to number the pages with a pen.

                              ANTHONY
                    Surely nothing.

The Manager opens Julia's desk's drawer and takes out a
simple appliance to put numbers on pages.

                              MANAGER
                    The archaic times are over, Mr.
                    Anthony!

The manager leaves the office.

INT. JOB OFFICE LOUNGE. DAY.

Anthony is sitting and waiting for his turn to speak to the
job office assistant.

                              ANTHONY (V.O.)
                    And yet they found out. I don't have
                    a promotion. Actually, I don't even
                    have a job. I registered with the
                    Employment Office. I feel that a new
                    chapter in my life is opening up. I
                    will get my benefit and I am going to
                    write a novel of my life during this
                    time.

Margaret enters Job office lounge. She notices Anthony.

                    MARGARET
          I thought that archivist job is for
          life?

                    ANTHONY
          Not when you are born to be a writer.

Fade out

Scandal

Written by

Katarzyna Adamus

Draft
information 1

Fade in

INT. PUB "LAST TURN". EVENING.

MICHAEL (30 years old man, well built and attractive) and
JANET (28 years old pretty female) are sitting at one of the
tables. They are drinking beer. There are a few empty
glasses and bottles on their table. It's late and as they
chat, people leave the venue one by one.

                    MICHAEL
          It's all about the proper scandal.
          Plus, it must show up in the news!
          Then I would be discovered as an
          artist.

                    JANET
          My mum keeps asking when are you
          going to propose. So, when?

                    MICHAEL
          I thought we are fine, as it is. Are
          we?

                    JANET
          You should find a proper job. Even in
          the factory. Be a man!

                    MICHAEL
          It's not me who supposed to change!
          Just listen to yourself! You should
          be supportive!

                    JANET
          Yes! I will support you. I have a
          perfect idea for a scandal. Marry
          this nut, who lives in the old
          forester's hut.

                    MICHAEL
          She is rather ugly...

                    JANET
          And older than you. I'm sure locals
          will visit you to buy a few of your
          paintings. Just out of curiosity. And
          you can expect only local fame. You
          are a horrible painter. By the way -
          we are over.

She stands up, trying to keep her balance.

                    MICHAEL
          Do you need a lift?

                    JANET
          Jonathan is on his way.

                    MICHAEL
          Jonathan? Your ex?

                    JANET
          You are my ex at the moment.

INT. PUB "LAST TURN". MORNING.

Michael and ALEXANDER (30 years old, looking like gym'
lover) are sitting at the table and eating portions of
English breakfast.

                    ALEXANDER
          So you split? Unbelievable. You were
          a couple for like two years?

                    MICHAEL
          Four. I need to make a proper
          scandal. Like a proper artist.

                    ALEXANDER
          You cannot make it on purpose.
          Firstly, it does not count,
          secondly...

                    MICHAEL
          I'm a good painter, but people do not
          want to buy anything from me. I need
          a scandal!

                    ALEXANDER
          This nut from forester's hut, she can
          help...

                    MICHAEL
          Why on Earth does everyone suggest
          her to me?

                    ALEXANDER
          She's a witch. She is doing the
          Tarot. Go and check out, how looks
          alike your future.

EXT. FOREST. DAY.

Michael is standing in the forest. It's very hot weather.
From the moss, who is covering the ground between the trees,
the steam goes up. It's quiet and beautiful.

                    THERESA (O.S.)
          Are you looking for me?

Michael turns around. For the first time, he sees THERESA.
She has a beautiful body, dressed in a sporty T-shirt and
leggings. Only one of her hands is longer than the other.
Her face is not beautiful, but she is not as ugly as
described by town people. Her foundation is very healthy and
glowing. Her eyes are sparking.

                    MICHAEL
          No. I got lost. I was looking for
          this nutter from the forester hut.
          She probably made some spell, I can't
          find the way back.

                    THERESA
          Not many people saw this place. And
          let it be like this. We don't want
          tourists to leave here trashes, do
          we? I will show you the way back.
          Follow me.

Michael follows the woman. They leave the beautiful place.

                    MICHAEL
          You are not afraid to go on your own
          to this forest?

                    THERESA
          I live here.

INT. GYM. DAY.

Michael and Alexander are sitting on the training benches,
situated next to each other. They are all covered in sweat
and drinking water.

                    ALEXANDER
          How is it possible you did not
          recognise her? She is as ugly as
          hell!

                    MICHAEL
          She is not a beauty, but she is not
          ugly as well.
                    (MORE)

                    MICHAEL (cont'd)
          Her eyes were so sparking, that I
          could not guess the colour of her
          eyes...

                    ALEXANDER
          Oh my God! She put a spell on you!
          Ha, ha! I would go with it to the
          local newspaper. You would have your
          scandal. I can see these headlines:
          "Her ugliness and handsome" or "She
          put a spell on me. I did not notice,
          she is ugly".

                    MICHAEL
          She's not ugly. Have you seen her?

                    ALEXANDER
          My mum wants to drive her to the hut
          each weekend for a tarot session. I
          see the witch on a regular basis. A
          few days ago she was still ugly. Did
          you eat any mushrooms in the forest?

                    MICHAEL
          She has a nice body...

                    ALEXANDER
          Oh my God!

He throws a towel at the Michael.

EXT. OUTSIDE OF ALEXANDER HOUSE. DAY.

Michael and Alexander are standing and lean against
Michael's jeep.

                    ALEXANDER
          This is crazy. I don't like to lie to
          my mum! I don't like to lie at all,
          so listen to this - this witch has
          turned your brain into the sponge.
          Soft one.

ALEXANDER'S MUM gets out of the house. She is around 60
years old. She approaches the men.

                    ALEXANDER'S MUM
          I don't know what's going on, but you
          have the same faces as ten years ago,
          when you broke the tractor engine.

                    ALEXANDER
        You don't want to know...

                    ALEXANDER'S MUM
        Broken car, huh? Let's go, she does
        not like to wait.

INT. FORESTER'S OLD HUT. KITCHEN. DAY.

Alexander and Michael are sitting in the kitchen and
drinking herbal tea.

                    MICHAEL
        Why it takes so long time?

                    ALEXANDER
        It lasts like a few seconds when are
        you with her. I have an idea. Give me
        your car keys.

                    MICHAEL
        Another of your crazy ideas?

From the hut's room, Alexander's Mum goes out.

                    ALEXANDER'S MUM
        It's your turn.

INT. FORESTER'S OLD HUT. LOUNGE. DAY.

Michael enters the room. Theresa is sitting at the table.
The window curtains cover the window. At the wooden and old
table, there are Tarot cards. Theresa is wearing a blue
dress and a black jacket. Her hair nicely combed.

                    MICHAEL
        Hi. Nice to meet you again. You look
        very nice...

                    THERESA
        If you want a discount, just ask. No
        need to lie.

                    MICHAEL
        I don't want a discount!

They hear the tyres shriek outside, as Alexander and
Alexander's Mum leave Michael on his own and go back to the
town.

INT. FORESTER'S OLD HUT. KITCHEN. EVENING.

Michael and Theresa are sitting at the kitchen table and drinking wine. They seem to like each other. They laugh. Michael touches the hand of Theresa.

                MICHAEL
       Did the Tarot cards say something
       about me?

                THERESA
       I can't use them too often. Once a
       day is maximum.

                MICHAEL
       Can I stay?

EXT. FOREST. DAY.

Michael and Theresa have a picnic in the place, where they met for the first time. They are hugging and kissing.

INT. FORESTER'S OLD HUT. KITCHEN. EVENING.

Michael and Theresa are drinking wine and looking at each other with love in their eyes. They listen to the music.

INT. FORESTER'S OLD HUT. BEDROOM. EARLY MORNING.

Michael and Theresa are sleeping in the bed, hugging each other. Suddenly Michael's phone rings. Michael wakes up and answers the phone.

              ALEXANDER
      You got your scandal! Come here!

                MICHAEL
       What happened?

              ALEXANDER
      You'd better meet me as soon as
      possible. You don't want to hear it
      from someone else...

Theresa wakes up. She listens to the conversation.

                MICHAEL
       Can I borrow your motorbike?

                         THERESA
          No. I know you will never come back.

                         MICHAEL
          Are you crazy? Of course, I will be
          back!

EXT. FOREST. MORNING.

Michael is driving a fast motorbike. He speeds up. Then he
slows down to take the hairpin turn. He slowly drives
through and speeds up.

INT. PUB "LAST TURN". MORNING.

Michael is sitting with Alexander at the table. On the
table, there are two empty beer glasses, two beers, and the
newspaper. On the front page, we see a headline "He left a
pregnant girlfriend and started a new life with the witch".

                         MICHAEL
          She was not pregnant! And she broke
          first!

                         ALEXANDER
          I don't know. But the newspapers are
          always right. According to town
          people, Janet is right. And you are a
          witch lover now.

                         MICHAEL
          Is it forbidden?

                         ALEXANDER
          Janet asked me to arrange the
          meeting. I did not know, she is not
          pregnant with you. Think about it.
          You were together for two years.

                         MICHAEL
          Four. I bet it's Jonathan's kid. She
          had a period when she broke with me.

The pub's door opens and Janet enters. She looks to be
around 4 months pregnant. She approaches Michael and
Alexander.

                         MICHAEL (cont'd)
          I need to go to the toilet. This
          morning beer...

Michael leaves the table and goes to the toilet. Janet sits at his place.

                    ALEXANDER
          I will speak to him. One moment.

Alexander gets up and follows Michael. Janet takes out something and pours to Michael's beer.

INT. PUB "LAST TURN". MORNING.

Alexander and Michael are coming back to the table. Janet is gone.

                    ALEXANDER
          Where is she?

                    MICHAEL
          I need one more beer! This situation
          is...

                    ALEXANDER
          You still did not finish your old
          one!

EXT. FOREST. HAIRPIN TURN. DAY.

Michael is driving back. He drives too fast. He sees everything blurry. He loses control over the motorbike. He has an accident.

EXT. FOREST. DAY.

In the place, where they first met, Theresa is laying on the autumn leaves. She is staring at the sky. Next to her, the newspaper with the article "Jealous witch caused and accident with ancient herbal poison. Police start an investigation. According to some witnesses, the witch was poisoning Michael B. on regular basis to get his attention. As far as we know, Michael wanted to get back to his pregnant girlfriend. There are also speculations, that he committed suicide because of the shame.".

Fade out

<u>Suggestion</u>

Written by
Katarzyna Adamus

Fade in

INT. KICKBOXING CLUB. AFTERNOON.

VICTORIA, short but very sexy brunette, punches and kicks a
punching bag. She looks well trained. TRAINER TOBY watches
her and comments.

                    TRAINER TOBY
               Leave something for your new
               boyfriend!

Victoria takes off punching gloves and throws them at
Trainer Toby's face. He got hit by surprise.

                    TRAINER TOBY (cont'd)
               OK, that's enough. We are finished
               also here. I don't want to see you at
               the training anymore!

INT. FLAT OF PETER AND VICTORIA. EVENING

VICTORIA, dressed in the gold evening dress, is chatting
with her boss on the phone.

                    VICTORIA
               Yes, I know. He sometimes behaves
               like a jerk. Yes, I will ask him to
               remove the car.

PETER gets out of the toilet. He is handsome and tall and
has an elegant suit on.

                    PETER
               Who is a jerk? Give me this phone!

Peter takes out the phone from Victoria's hand.

                    PETER (cont'd)
               Listen to me! I am not going to
               remove the car! I have permission
               from the city council. It will stay
               there, you want it or not.

He gives back the phone to Victoria, who continue to chat
with the boss.

                    VICTORIA
               Yes? I can't do this! Honestly! He is
               my boyfriend... Hello? Hello?

She puts the phone into an evening bag.

                    PETER
          What did he say?

                    VICTORIA
          I can not repeat it.

Peter starts to laugh.

                    PETER
          I did not know you have a feminine
          side and try to play games.

                    VICTORIA
          What do you mean?

                    PETER
          Nothing! Ready? The taxi is waiting!

They are leaving the flat.

INT. HOTEL. BALLROOM. EVENING.

Peter's company workers are having an annual party in the
hotel ballroom. People dance or chat. Victoria sits at the
table, alone. Peter is chatting and dancing with a blonde
woman. They finish the dance. Peter approaches Victoria.

                    PETER
          Why are you that boring?

                    VICTORIA
          Boring? Yesterday I demolished all
          buildings with one hit! And last week
          I did a selective demolition,
          removing just one wall at the top
          floor of ...

                    PETER
          Shhh! Quiet! There are mostly
          intelligent people here. And by the
          way - you broke the crane. If I was
          your boss, I would fire you.

                    VICTORIA
          You will never be my boss!

                    PETER
          Are you sure? Maybe I am already? Who
          pays most of the bills? You and your
          blue-collar salary?

                         VICTORIA
              I can move out if it is a problem.

Peter takes out of his pocket a small jewellery box. He
shows discreetly a ring to Victoria.

                         PETER
              Be nice, so maybe I will become your
              boss!

                         VICTORIA
              I suggest you, don't piss me off.

She gets up. Peter grabs her hand.

                         PETER
              Better be nice. There are lots of
              nice girls here.

Victoria breaks away from Peter's grip. She goes to the
toilet.

INT. HOTEL'S TOILET. EVENING.

Victoria is breathing heavily. She looks at her face in the
mirror. She tries to smile, but only a twist appears on her
face. She looks at her cheek. We can see a bit of bruise
through the makeup. Victoria takes out the foundation and
corrects her make up.

INT. HOTEL. EVENING.

Victoria enters the ballroom, just to see Peter kissing with
the blonde woman during a dance. Victoria freeze for few
seconds then she leaves the hotel.

INT. FLAT OF PETER AND VICTORIA. LATE EVENING.

Victoria is sitting at the kitchen table and drinking wine.
Her phone rings. Victoria picks it with hesitation.

                         VICTORIA
              Yes?

                         PETER
              Where are you?

                         VICTORIA
              I'm at home.

                         PETER
               In my flat?

Victoria does not answer.

                         PETER (cont'd)
               We will talk when I am back. You
               screwed it this time.

                         VICTORIA
               When you are back?

                         PETER
               When I'm back. I have to work on some
               projects in my office.

                         VICTORIA
               Yeah, right!

                         PETER
               We need to discuss your behaviour
               again.

Victoria puts the phone away and starts to drink.

EXT. OUTSIDE OF THE VICTORIA'S WORK OFFICE. MORNING.

Victoria, dressed in labour clothes and high vest, is
chatting with her BOSS. He is tall, bald, in his '50s.

                         VICTORIA
               I can't do this! He would kill me!

                         BOSS
               Law is on our side. And we have
               insurance.

                         VICTORIA
               He wanted to propose yesterday. It's
               just me...

                         BOSS
               It's not you. Do what I say.

                         VICTORIA
               I will think about it.

INT. FLAT OF PETER AND VICTORIA. EVENING

Victoria, still in working clothes, is eating a microwave
dish. She looks tired. Peter enters the flat.

                         PETER
          Where have you been? With whom?

                         VICTORIA
          I should ask this question!

                         PETER
          But I was first! OK, honey. Let's not
          argue. I will forgive you this time.
          What's for dinner?

Victoria looks confused.

                         VICTORIA
          The blonde one can't cook?

                         PETER
          Honey, you are the only one! You know
          this!

He takes out the box and gets on one knee.

                         PETER (cont'd)
          Will you marry me?

                         VICTORIA
          I have to come back to work!

                         PETER
          Answer! Answer!

Victoria stays silent. She bows her head. Dark hair falls on
her face.

                         PETER (cont'd)
          Answer!

Peter grabs Victoria's hair. She tries to free herself.

                         PETER (cont'd)
          Be cool! Just answer!

Victoria kicks Peter. Surprised, he loses the grip. Victoria
gets away.

                         PETER (cont'd)
          You will have to come back, darling.
          Then we will talk. Oh yes! We will
          talk.

EXT. STREET NEXT TO THE FLAT OF PETER AND VICTORIA. LATE
EVENING.

The piloting vehicle drives with the yellow lights on.
Behind him, in big demolishing crane, Victoria drives. They
approach the only car left on the street. Victoria's Boss
watches this from the pavement.

> BOSS
> Just do it, girl!

Victoria is next to the car. She looks at the Boss. He nods
his head. Victoria switches something in the crane. The end
of the crane lands precisely on the car, crashing it
completely.

> BOSS (cont'd)
> Good girl! My girl!

INT. COURT. DAY.

Victoria's Boss is talking, answering THE JUDGE question.

> BOSS
> The crane was broken. We asked all
> owners to remove their cars. It was a
> difficult operation. We are very
> sorry for the damage. We are fully
> insured. The insurance should cover
> the cost.

> THE JUDGE
> It is not that simple. What is the
> personal relationship between you and
> Ms. Veronica Palmer?

> BOSS
> She is my daughter.

> THE JUDGE
> Was she qualified to do this job?

> BOSS
> She has the best exam results from my
> team. She is even better than me. She
> has a gift!

Peter starts to shout.

> PETER
> She and gift! She even can not cook
> properly. Only microwave meals.
> (MORE)

                    PETER (cont'd)
Microwave meals for whole the whole
month.

Peter changes his voice, shadowing the voice of Victoria.

                    PETER (cont'd)
"I'm tired."

                    THE JUDGE
And what is the relation between Ms.
Palmer and Mr. Peter Martin?

                    BOSS
It is her lousy... I mean it is her
boyfriend.

                    THE JUDGE
Mind your language, Mr. Palmer. I
would like now to hear the statement
of the technician.

THE TECHNICIAN swears on the Bible. The Judge asks him the
first question.

                    THE JUDGE (cont'd)
Are you related to any of the people
in this room?

                    THE TECHNICIAN
No.

                    THE JUDGE
What are the results of your
investigation?

                    THE TECHNICIAN
The crane was broken. It was fixed by
mobile mechanics, but it looks like
it broke again. We are lucky it
finished like this.

                    THE JUDGE
Mr. Martin, please stand up.

Peter stands up.

                    THE JUDGE (cont'd)
Mr. Martin, 1000 pounds penalty for
not obeying the rules, and not
removing the car. Mr. Palmer?

Boss stands up.

                         THE JUDGE (cont'd)
               You will need to cover the damage. We
               might also do further investigation
               regarding the whole procedures of
               this operation. At the moment you are
               dismissed.

INT. FLAT OF PETER AND VICTORIA. EVENING

Peter sits at the coffee table checking something on the
laptop. Suddenly he starts to laugh.

                         PETER
               Looks like someone forgot about these
               photos. But not me!

INT. HOTEL ROOM. EVENING.

Victoria sits on the bed and watches TV. Her phone rings.
She answers.

                         TRAINER TOBY
               Did you lose your mind?

                         VICTORIA
               Yes, I lost it in the moment I
               answered this phone! What do you
               want? Do you think I will jump again
               in your arms?

                         TRAINER TOBY
               This would be great, but... When did
               you check your Facebook account?

Victoria gets of bed immediately.

                         VICTORIA
               Oh shit! What did he post?

                         TRAINER TOBY
               Don't worry, I will take care of him.
               Just remove the post.

Victoria puts aside a phone. She checks her Facebook account
and starts to cry.

INT. FLAT OF PETER AND VICTORIA. LATE EVENING.

Through the open balcony door, the end of the crane is
coming slowly. Peter is sleeping on the sofa.

His open laptop is on the coffee table. The end of the crane
is now exactly over the table. It gets higher, just to land
few seconds later on the laptop.

INT. COURT. DAY.

The same judge is looking with a serious face at present
people. Peter is sitting next to his solicitor. Victoria,
Boss (her father), and their solicitor are sitting together.
They do not see Toby, who enters the courtroom, and sits
behind them.

                    THE JUDGE
          Mr. Martin, did I overheard or you
          confirm saying, that you put pictures
          of Miss Palmer with explicit content
          on social media?

                    PETER
          She did it! She is crazy! She went
          with her favourite bulldozer after
          me! She should be locked!

                    THE JUDGE
          Mr. Martin, did you see who was a
          driver of this vehicle, which
          according to your statement entered
          your third floor flat and damaged
          your laptop and table?

                    PETER
          Vehicle? She drove this broken crane
          probably.

                    THE JUDGE
          Miss Palmer, did you drive the crane?

                    VICTORIA
          No. You can not drive the crane. We
          have different kinds of machines, but
          cranes are still.

Peter starts to threaten Victoria, with a low voice, so the
Judge can not hear him.

                    PETER
          Do you want a war with me? You will
          get it!

                    THE JUDGE
          I will ask now a few questions to a
          POLICE INVESTIGATOR.

POLICE INVESTIGATOR gets up from the back row. He swears on the Bible.

                    THE JUDGE (cont'd)
          Are you in any relation with any of
          person present in this room?

                    POLICE INVESTIGATOR
          Yes, the drawing artist is my
          fiancee.

                    THE JUDGE
          Please tell us the outcome of your
          investigation.

                    POLICE INVESTIGATOR
          The damage was made inside of the
          building on the third floor. None of
          the neighbours reported seeing crane,
          I mean, any suspicious machine.
          However, we found some bits of yellow
          paint, which fits to the paint of Mr.
          Palmer's company's machines.

                    THE JUDGE
          Does it fit it exactly?

                    POLICE INVESTIGATOR
          It is a minor case. We do not have
          funds for further investigation. It
          is expensive. It could be any
          machine.

                    THE JUDGE
          Can we check CCTV footage?

                    POLICE INVESTIGATOR
          We do not have CCTV everywhere.
          Please state from which cameras you
          would like footage and I will do the
          best I can. However we do not keep
          footage forever, and it has been two
          months already...

                    THE JUDGE
          Mr. Palmer, knowing, how costly it
          will be for the society to get to
          know the truth, would you like to
          share something with us?

                    TRAINER TOBY
          I did it.

                    VICTORIA
          No, It was me.

                    BOSS
          They both lie. It was me.

                    POLICE INVESTIGATOR
          Looks like we have three suspects.

                    THE JUDGE
          Remember about the owe.

Peter looks really annoyed.

                    PETER
          Lock all of them, they are all
          dangerous!

                    THE JUDGE
          A question to all three suspects: did
          you drive the machine altogether?

                    TRAINER TOBY
          They got an alibi. She was in the
          hotel, he was drinking with his mate.
          It was me.

                    VICTORIA
          Thank you, Toby, but I can take care
          of myself. It was me! Toby was with
          his new girlfriend.

                    TRAINER TOBY
          I do not have a girlfriend.

                    VICTORIA
          Ah, yes. I forgot you are careful
          with naming.

The Judge looks at her papers. She clears her throat then
says.

                    THE JUDGE
          According to the law cooperation of
          three persons would count as
          organized crime. However, the object
          was of low value. Noone also saw the
          crane, I mean the demolishing
          machine. If you just could explain,
          how did you do?

> BOSS
> I was drinking with a friend. It is
> quite strong alibi, we were thrown
> out of the pub and banned for the
> next four weeks.

> VICTORIA
> I was in the hotel. You can check
> CCTV.

> TRAINER TOBY
> I was with someone. A female.

The judge looks confused at present. Then she asks Police
investigator.

> THE JUDGE
> Do we have any basis to accuse anyone
> here?

> POLICE INVESTIGATOR
> No. We are not that good as they show
> in Hollywood movies.

The Judge hits with the hammer onto her table.

> THE JUDGE
> All dismissed until further notice.

> PETER
> What does it mean? It is her? She is
> evil! And her eyes! Look at her.
> These are devil eyes!

He takes his binder and throws at Victoria, hitting her in
the head. Victoria jumps at Peter, punching and kicking him.
He looks shocked.

> PETER (cont'd)
> Your Honor! It's the best example!

INT. PETER'S BOSS OFFICE. DAY.

PETER'S BOSS is looking at photos of Peter. On one picture
Peter is in chains, just in the underwear. On the second
one, the content is more explicit.

Loud knocking to the door. Peter enters the office with a
smile on his face.

PETER
Finally! I was almost certain you
want to fire me!

PETER'S BOSS
It's not yet decided. But the
situation is tricky.

He shows pictures to Peter.

PETER'S BOSS (cont'd)
You understand our situation. As
policy makers, we have to care about
our reputation...

Peter's smile is gone.

PETER
Well, the amount of five years'
salary as a redundancy payment maybe
would satisfy me. Otherwise, I will
have to publish these photos. You
know, I would like to have a big
coming out!

Peter's Boss tears the photos in anger.

PETER'S BOSS
You will never get a job in this
city!

EXT. OUTSIDE OF THE VICTORIA'S WORK OFFICE. AFTERNOON.

Victoria leaves her workplace after the day shift. She is in
her work clothes and a high vest jacket. She walks the
pavement with her head high. Suddenly she hears a whistle.
She turns around just to see Peter following her in his new
car. It's even more expensive than the last one.

PETER
Did you miss me?

Victoria firstly cowers. Then she straightens her posture.

VICTORIA
Get out and find out!

PETER
Come on, get in. We need to celebrate
my small victory. I became overday
millionaire!

                         VICTORIA
              Yes, why not!

She gets into the car to surprise Peter.

                         PETER
              I was joking! You a simply a bitch!
              Just after my money!

                         VERONICA
              I just wanted to advise how to spend
              them.

Peter starts to laugh.

                         PETER
              Yeah? How?

Veronica grabs his head and knocks it on the driving wheel.
Peter looks at her shocked and surprised. Veronica punches
him straight in the nose. It cracks and we see it's badly
broken. Veronica starts to beat him in the nose even more.

From the office, Boss is going out. He jumps to the car and
drags Veronica out. At this time Peter's face is covered in
blood. The nose is badly damaged.

                         VERONICA
              How? You will need all of them for a
              nose job!

Fade out

<u>The seller</u>

Written by

Katarzyna Adamus

Draft
information
2

Fade in

INT. HOTEL ROOM. EARLY MORNING. NOVEMBER.

JACK, the 30 years old man, is sitting at a bed, with his
face hidden behind the palms. Suddenly he grabs his phone,
laying on the bed, and starts to call MARGARET.

                    JACK
          Hi... No, I do not want you back,
          don't worry.

                    MARGARET
          What happened this time?

                    JACK
          I'm OK. I got a job!

                    MARGARET
          Yeah? Tell me about it!

                    JACK
          I am a seller. This week I am selling
          books.

                    MARGARET
          Ha, ha! Did you become a bookseller?
          You were supposed to be a writer,
          weren't you?

                    JACK
          I got just a few minutes. Tell me
          more about your research, about these
          nuts...

                    MARGARET
          They do not have that much
          hallucinogen effect. You would be
          better with simple...

                    JACK
          I am talking about these changing
          colour of teeth into the black!

                    MARGARET
          Betel nuts. You are nuts as well!

Jack dials another phone number and calls CAMILA.

                    JACK
          Hello darling... No worries I am not
          after you anymore.

                    CAMILA
          Are you again in this place?

                    JACK
          I am at work. I mean, in the hotel.
          Listen, could you do me a favour and
          buy something in this Asian shop next
          to you?

                    CAMILA
          Yes.

                    JACK
          Just a packet of betel nuts. And
          please send it as soon as possible.
          One day delivery. I will pay you
          back.

                    CAMILA
          Yeah... Nevermind. I will send it to
          you.

EXT. SMALL VILLAGE ROAD. MORNING. A FEW HOURS LATER.

Jack and VICTOR are walking on the road's berm. It is
raining. Jack is wearing a thin coat. Victor is jumping over
the puddles. Jack is sidestepping them, sometimes his foot
is ending up in the water.

                    JACK
          Don't you think we are some kind of
          cult?

                    VICTOR
          No! We are in direct sales
          representation!

                    JACK
          Just listen to this. Each month, we
          are transported to different parts of
          Poland. Just not to make any bonds
          with other people. From the morning
          till late afternoon, like some
          slavers, we are trying to sell goods
          to the incredulous residents of towns
          and villages. So our time is taken
          from us. After work, we do not have
          free time. We need to gather in the
          hotel. The company covers the costs
          of accommodation. Who does it
          nowadays? And this gong!

                    VICTOR
          You are jealous because you never hit
          the sales target to hit the gong! And
          we have a great manager!

                    JACK
          Don't say you like his bullshit talk?

                    VICTOR
          He's great, man. He really is. He was
          studying sales with the best! You
          should listen to him more carefully!

                    JACK
          I do not doubt his skills. Just the
          products!

                    VICTOR
          What's wrong with them?

                    JACK
          Do you really think that our
          orthopaedic pillows will straighten
          peasant's hunches and curvatures, and
          that juicers will add vitamins to
          their organisms, whose main feed is
          potato, and that the books will
          evolve abstract thinking in a tractor
          driver's mind?

                    VICTOR
          Your problem is that you think you
          are better! Do you think you are
          better? For example better than me?

They are passing houses. Few small dogs run out from one of
the yards and attack them.

                    VICTOR (cont'd)
          What the hell?

                    JACK
          You see, I will explain to you these
          dogs behaviour.

One of the dogs starts to pluck Jack's trousers.

                    VICTOR
          Yes! Explain this! You must be a bad
          man if dogs do not like you!

                    JACK
          Village barkers' manners in the post-
          communist villages are different from
          city curs, walked by the
          distinguished old ladies. Bigger dogs
          are always barking lazily from the
          inland of backyards, on chains linked
          to dog houses. Smaller barkers are
          enjoying freedom and using it to get
          rid of their inferiority complex.
          The biggest ambition of the village
          dogs is to pluck the turn-ups of the
          door-to-door seller's trousers.
          Especially, the turn-ups of the door-
          to door seller who suffers from
          depression.

                    VICTOR
          So you are crazy! Ha, ha, ha!

The dogs leave Jack's trousers and start to attack Victor.

                    VICTOR (cont'd)
          Go away! Good dogs!

The dogs start to bark even more loudly. Victor starts to
run, the dogs chase him. Jack continues to walk.

                    JACK
          You deserved this, Mr. Smart!

From one of the houses, ELENA is getting out. She is a sexy
blonde. She looks worried. She notices Jack.

                    ELENA
          Did you sell something today?

                    JACK
          Yes, one book, to the old lady.
          Probably she bought it because of the
          greediness to just have it and the
          lack of any shops in a few miles'
          area. In more favourable conditions,
          this old lady would probably have
          become a shopaholic.

                    ELENA
          Oh my God! I can't be worse! Mark
          said, that if someone will get worse
          results than you...

                    JACK
        I had a dream that I murdered him
        with the orthopaedic pillow. Or was
        it this night our gong?

                    ELENA
        He gave you a job!

                    JACK
        He is nonsense!

                    ELENA
        If you would start to smile, maybe
        you would sell something!

                    JACK
        After the last border control, I know
        that the quality of my smile is poor.
        During the procedure of comparing my
        face with the passport picture, I
        tried the best door-to-door seller's
        smile. As a result, the officer
        checked the passport in detail using
        some proper vetting.

                    ELENA
        Sorry, Jack, I prefer to work on my
        own. You are too scary, and you have
        no energy. I can't lose my income,
        sorry.

Elena is leaving him, and going in the opposite direction.

                    JACK
        Bitch! I will show you who is a
        better seller!

Jack enters the house, which Elena left. The door opens a
WOMAN, who is perfectly dressed and does not look like a
typical housewife.

                    JACK (cont'd)
        I am representing a Marketpol
        company. Do you have a while?

                    WOMAN
        It depends for what…

A Woman puts one of her hands on the hip.

                    JACK
        We are doing some market research
        about reading habits in this village.
                    (MORE)

                        JACK (cont'd)
          Could you please answer a few
          questions?

                        WOMAN
          Yes. I can talk about books. Please
          get inside.

INT. WOMAN'S HOUSE. LOUNGE.DAY.

Jack and the Woman are sitting at the table and drinking
tea.

                        WOMAN
          I read around three books per week.
          Mainly the Nobel prize winners'
          books. Our library is well-equipped.
          But the Clancy is next to Camus, and
          "The Vatican Cellars" is between the
          books on religious studies. Well, I
          try not to complain.

                        JACK
          Nobel prize winners... Well, I have a
          few romance books, encyclopaedias,
          and epic book...

The Woman looks at shown books and takes "A small
encyclopaedia of reptiles" in her hand.

                        WOMAN
          This should be useful. You know, the
          bricklayers make few fudges and the
          floor is not even. I need something
          nice to put under one desk's leg. And
          this book…I can even read it… You may
          add this thin romance book, under the
          second table leg.

Jack collects money and leaves the house.

EXT. SMALL VILLAGE ROAD. MORNING. A FEW MINUTES LATER.

Elena is just leaving the neighbour's house.

                        JACK
          I just sold two!

Elena is staring at him.

                        ELENA
          I do not believe you.

                    JACK
          Yes, I know also someone else, who
          can buy more!

                    ELENA
          Liar!

INT. SMALL VILLAGE LIBRARY. DAY. A FEW MINUTES LATER.

Jack enters the library, just to witness an argument between
CLIENT - young blonde in animal pattern coat, and LIBRARIAN,
older woman in modest clothes.

                    CLIENT
          I have not borrowed this book!

                    LIBRARIAN
          The card is on your account.

                    CLIENT
          But I have not borrowed it. Do I look
          like a chicken raising fan?

                    LIBRARIAN
          We can't do anything. You will be
          able to borrow books, but first, you
          need to return "Chicken raising".

The Librarian asks Jack.

                    LIBRARIAN (cont'd)
          How can I help?

Jack takes out the books from his bag. When Librarian
notices the colourful covers of the romance books, a smile
pops up on her face.

                    LIBRARIAN (cont'd)
          I just need to ask the manager!

She goes behind the books shelves and comes back after a
while.

                    LIBRARIAN (cont'd)
          I will take ten romance books!

EXT. OUTSIDE OF THE LIBRARY. DAY. A FEW MINUTES LATER.

The Client is waiting outside of the library.

                    CLIENT
          I swear I did not borrow this fucking
          book. What do you have to sell?

Jack shows her last three romance books.

                    CLIENT (cont'd)
          I will take all of them. You are a
          city man? You don't know how boring
          is here!

Jack collects money.

                    JACK
          Yes, I bet most of the people are
          concerned about raising chickens
          only.

INT. HOTEL LOUNGE. THE NEXT DAY. LATE AFTERNOON.

Jack enters the hotel and collects a small parcel from the
reception. Then he is going into the conference room.

INT. CONFERENCE ROOM IN THE HOTEL. A FEW MINUTES LATER. LATE
AFTERNOON.

Jack enters the conference room and rings a small gong.

Victor and Elena are already inside.

                    VICTOR
          No bullshit! You could not hit the
          record! Not today! Not here! Not the
          second day in the row!

MARK, a manager, is standing next to the board.

                    MARK
          Looks like we have a new sales
          leader!

Jack approaches Mark and hands him a packet of betel nuts.

                    MARK (cont'd)
          What is it? A bribe?

                    JACK
          It is some drug. It has similar
          qualities to nicotine.

                    MARK
          A drug is not a bribe! Did you
          finally managed to memorise our sales
          scripts? Please repeat after me
          "offer of a lifetime"...

                    JACK
          Offer... Life - life- lifetime
          offer..

                    MARK
          A child in kindergarten would
          memorise this text faster! And you
          are working for us for three months!

                    JACK
          I just have a selective memory!

                    MARK
          Go back to your seat.

He starts to speak to all sellers.

                    MARK (cont'd)

          So! We are ready to start?

Mark takes the packet and opens it.

                    MARK (cont'd)
          How kind! I love nuts!

All sellers take their places at the conference table.

                    MARK (cont'd)
          Today we are going to refresh our
          knowledge about the types of clients.
          Who remembers the types of clients?

                    VICTOR
          Those who know that they need the
          product, and those who do not know
          this yet.

                    MARK
          Yes, that's correct. We like the
          first type of clients the most, but I
          am telling you - the client, who gets
          to know that he needs the product is
          an even better client!

The sellers start whispering and commenting quietly.

                              MARK (cont'd)
                    So, how do we convince a client, that
                    he needs a product?

He starts biting the nuts.

                              VICTOR
                    We say about the qualities of the
                    product!

                              ELENA
                    We say that the neighbour had bought
                    it!

Mark nods, intensively chewing nuts.

                              MARK
                    But what is most important?

The silence begins. All sellers are looking at each other,
wrinkling their foreheads and trying to find out a
satisfactory reply.
Marc is watching all of them, eating another betel nut.

                              MARK (cont'd)
                    The most important is a
                    demonstration!

Suddenly his eyes blur. The packet falls from his hand. From
the throat of the manager a deep strange sound comes. He
falls on his knees.

                              VICTOR
                    Is it a new technique?

                              ELENA
                    The client will buy it?

The manager falls over his side. Through his half-closed
eyes, they can see only the whiteness. From his mouth, a
small stream of saliva comes out.

                              JACK
                    I think we need an ambulance! Who
                    still has a credit on his phone?

                              VICTOR
                    I will call. I already have had a bad
                    day.

INT. HOTEL ROOM. EVENING. A FEW HOURS LATER.

Jack is texting someone on his phone. The phone starts to
ring.

> JACK
> Listen, is there something I should
> know about these nuts? The manager...
> Mark... He is dead!

> MARGARET
> Oh my God! How many did he eat?

> JACK
> Few... Maybe more...

> MARGARET
> You can write a book in prison!

> JACK
> It could be something else! I'm not a
> murderer! You are! You were thinking
> it is for me, weren't you?

INT. THE CONFERENCE ROOM. NEXT DAY MORNING.

The sellers are listening to the NEW MANAGER.

> NEW MANAGER
> Death will not destroy our success!

POLICEMAN is entering the conference room.

> POLICEMAN
> Our pathologist discovered a new
> toxic substance in the dead body of
> your-ex boss. Do you have any useful
> information?

EXT. OUTSIDE OF THE HOTEL. A FEW HOURS LATER.

Policeman is leaving the hotel, leading arrested, Jack.

INT. POLICE ROOM. A FEW HOURS LATER.

PSYCHIATRIST is talking with Jack.

                    JACK
          It was a joke! I mean it supposed to
          be a joke! The nuts supposed to turn
          his teeth into black colour!

                    PSYCHIATRIST
          Do you have any other problems than
          depression? Do you hear voices for
          example?

Psychiatrist nods his head and kicks Jack's leg under the
table.

                    JACK
          Yes, I can hear some voices
          sometimes... Like you for example...

The Psychiatrist kicks him again.

                    JACK (cont'd)
          And all kinds of others... Yes!
          Definitely, I can hear voices.
          Sometimes even in my head, for
          example, my muse voice.

The Psychiatrist starts to write a report, speaking aloud
the content.

                    PSYCHIATRIST
          Man of 30 years, reported depression
          problem and hearing voices in his
          head. He also reported that his sales
          company is a kind of cult. Man is
          talking a lot about problems with the
          dogs. He thinks that his smile is
          causing him problems. I suspect
          paranoid schizophrenia. This man
          should be sectioned for a few months
          and the medicines should be provided.

                    JACK
          Sectioned? Again? I did not want to
          do anything this time!

The psychiatrist stops to write.

                    JACK (cont'd)
          Ah yes. Happy end in the asylum.
          Thank you, doctor.

INT. PSYCHIATRIC WARD. PSYCHIATRIST'S OFFICE. DAY.

Psychiatrist and Jack are sitting on the chairs. Between
them there is a desk. Psychiatrist is writing report on the
paper.

                    PSYCHIATRIST
          That's interesting. Interesting. But
          just between us. I have a new
          medicine to be tested on few
          volunteers. We do not know possible
          side effects yet.

                    JACK
          I will be OK with some lavender tea
          for my nerves.

                    PSYCHIATRIST
          Do you think that this tea will help
          you to cope with the prison routine?

                    JACK
          That new medicine... How long I
          should take it?

                    PSYCHIATRIST
          Six months and you will be able to
          get back to the society. Maybe one
          year.

                    JACK
          One year. One year!

                    PSYCHIATRIST
          You can do a singing class in this
          time. We have a good teacher.

                    JACK
          Can I take a ballet class?

Fade out

Printed in Great Britain
by Amazon

78645266R00081